CRYPTID CURRENCY

Josh Berliner

ISBN: 9781963832129 (paperback) / 9781963832235 (ebook)
LCCN: 2024951571
Copyright © 2025 by Josh Berliner
Cover illustration © 2025 by Ian Bristow

Printed in the United States of America.

Names, characters, and incidents depicted in this book are products of the author's imagination or are used fictitiously. Any resemblance to actual events, locales, organizations, or persons, living or dead, is entirely coincidental and beyond the intent of the author or the publisher.

All rights reserved. No part of this book may be reproduced or transmitted in any form or by any means, electronic or mechanical, including photocopying, recording or by any information storage or retrieval system without written permission of the publisher, except for the inclusion of brief quotations in a review.

NO AI TRAINING: Without in any way limiting the author's [and publisher's] exclusive rights under copyright, any use of this publication to "train" generative artificial intelligence (AI) technologies to generate text is expressly prohibited. The author reserves all rights to license uses of this work for generative AI training and development of machine learning language models.

Kinkajou Press
9 Mockingbird Hill Rd
Tijeras, New Mexico 87059
info@kinkajoupress.com
www.kinkajoupress.com

This book is dedicated to my wife, Amber, whose love and support sustains me, revives me, and empowers me.

Special thanks are owed to the members of the Ludington Writers group. Without your feedback, guidance, and honesty, this would not have been possible.

Prologue

August 18th, 1901

An otherwise ordinary afternoon in the town of Raspberry Hill, Pennsylvania was interrupted by the emergence of a black cat from her home at the Curiosity Shop. Now, this was not an unusual occurrence by anyone's standards but the cat herself—who preferred a warm blanket to anywhere else in the universe—but what was noteworthy about her was the gold coin she clutched between her teeth.

Her goal—something absolutely vital—would require it.

The cat passed the drugstore, and the druggist took passive notice of the moneyed feline but didn't devote much thought to her. He was not the sort of man to question things he didn't understand. Therefore, he didn't question much of anything.

She continued in her mission up the street. Past the library, the police station, and the town square, where a crowd of people witnessed her. No one wanted to be the first to point out her strangeness, until a small child relieved them of the burden by remarking, "There's a kitty with a coin!"

"No, sweetheart," her mother reassured her—and by extension, everyone else. "It's just your imagination. Cats don't use money."

Spared from the grim fate of appearing foolish, the clandestine gawkers could return to their self-imposed ignorance.

Josh Berliner

The cat leapt across the windowsill of the pub, where she was spotted by one of its patrons. His bleary eyes registered her, then scanned over to his liquid meal, then slid back over to her. Perhaps it was finally time to rethink his lifestyle. Better order another glass to make sure.

She hopped from the windowsill to that of her destination, the market. Letting herself in through the open window, she crept over to the grocer, who was taking inventory of the apples and bananas. He felt a tug on his pant leg and found a midnight-black cat with moonlight-yellow eyes staring expectantly at him.

"The usual, I presume?" he asked.

"Meow," said the cat.

He extracted a fresh filet of trout from the ice box and gave it to the cat. She dropped the coin in his hand, and the transaction was complete. It was an arrangement the grocer had become accustomed to, and who was he to question it? After all, a customer was a customer, even if said customer walked on four legs.

Fish in mouth, the cat dashed down the street to her home. She let herself in through an open window on the second story, where the Curiosity Shop's owner, Levi Mortenson, had his apartment. Mealtime required an audience, so she searched for him in the bedroom, in the washroom, and eventually found him at the checkout counter in the shop downstairs.

The old man was seated behind the cash register, hunched over a ledger, muttering to himself, and scribbling around with his pen. That was a human matter, and she had far more important things to do, like eat trout.

"It's no use... no use," he grumbled as the cat laid down on top of his work. "Hrmph. Ysabel, I can't see what I'm doing."

She, naturally, said nothing. Whatever he was doing couldn't possibly be more important than paying attention to her while she ate her breakfast.

He sighed, "It's no good anyway. No matter how I add it up, I can't make it balance. In any case, it's not going to be *enough.* He'll *be here in only two weeks' time, and there's no way I can get more together to pay* him. *I could go and—no, I couldn't make the journey by myself. I wouldn't survive. This is it. I think it's the end for me."*

Mortenson leaned back in his chair, which groaned to match the feeling that festered within him. The cat snacked away and only paused to lick her lips. Whatever the old man was worried about was a human affair, and therefore not worthy of her consideration.

He continued to ponder, "Perhaps if I got some help, I could pull it off. On second thought, it would be far too risky. I don't know anyone who would be able to handle it. Sigh... If only there were someone I could trust..."

Chapter 1

SINCE YOU'VE DECIDED TO read this book, you must have heard the name Gunnar Shuck and the rumors that surround me. If you haven't, you are in for the surprise of your life. So many others are curious to know the truth of what happened. Not a week goes by when I don't receive a stack of letters asking all sorts of questions:

Did I really work for Levi Mortenson at the Curiosity Shop in Raspberry Hill, Pennsylvania? Is it true that I helped him capture all manner of incredible creatures? Is magic actually real?

For a long time, I ignored these inquiries. Few could be trusted to know what truly occurred, and anyone I did trust with the knowledge refused to believe it anyway. Over time, rumors have become misinformation—and that, by far, is worse—so I think the time is finally right to set the record straight. The magic, the peril, and the mystery will finally be revealed to you in detail, patient reader.

My story begins before all of that, however.

I was ten years old when I had my first encounter with the paranormal. It was on a hot, sticky summer night at my parents' farm in Shroud's Creek, Tennessee in 1897. Whether or not anyone believed me then or will now, I am convinced that what I saw was real and that it changed the entire course of my life. You may proceed assured, generous reader, that your narrator is fully reliable.

I am the first of Luke and Mary Shuck's children, and the older brother to two sisters, Eleanor and Rosemary. At that time Ellie was beginning to learn farm work and had just started school. Rosie was still a toddler, taking on the primary responsibilities of terrorizing chickens. I had my hands full with my schoolwork and helping Pa on the farm.

My father was a Salt-of-the-Earth type of man, the product of a rough and desperate childhood. He was self-disciplined, cautious with money, and defiantly proud of the modest farm that had been in our family for five generations. His no-nonsense attitude made him an effective farmer and patriarch of the family, at the cost of a gruff exterior that could make it hard to get close to him.

The man was a pincher of pennies and eyebrows. The folds of his wallet scarcely parted, and neither did the bushy orange eyebrows that rested above his sapphire-blue eyes. This was caused by decades of difficult farm work and struggling to make ends meet. It wasn't all bad, since a lifetime of toiling on the farm had given him the stocky, muscular build of an Olympic wrestler.

Ma was the true brain behind the Shuck farm. She had long, beautiful tangerine hair which draped behind her, reaching her knees. This wasn't as impressive as it may sound at first, since she could be described as "petite," a word people use when they don't want to offend short people. There's a trend for people of lesser height to make up for it in ferocity of spirit, and Ma was obviously not an exception to that.

She shared Pa's attitude of stark realism but possessed a cunning strategic mind that allowed her to see exactly what needed to be done to make the farm work. Many such women exist, but Ma had the advantage of a husband who understood that her shrewd intellect was not to be held back by any man's stubborn pride.

My sisters and I were near copies of our parents. We inherited the shortness of our mother, the blue eyes of our father, and the fiery red hair of both. In a town full of brown-haired, brown-eyed, average folks, we certainly stood out.

Shroud's Creek was the kind of town where your next-door neighbor lived a mile away from you, and even though you might occasionally share a passing word with them at the general store once a week, everyone somehow knew everyone else's business. That store, town hall, and the church—which doubled as the schoolhouse on weekdays—were the only properties that were not farms.

The Shuck Family farm was the smallest farm in Shroud's Creek. Both the farmhouse and the single barn were old, drafty, and small, but they were ours. Our annual crop of wheat and corn, as well as our keeping of one milk cow and many chickens, earned enough to get by on. Ends met, but being the smallest farm meant that you were implied to be the worst.

Every community needs someone to lie at the bottom of the heap—so to speak—on which to build its social foundation. As the de facto poorest family in Shroud's Creek, that was us. Many of the townsfolk would fake politeness to our faces but then laugh at the dusty, skinny, red-headed Shucks. Everyone needs *someone* to look down on and believe they are superior to.

"Well, hi Gunnar," they'd call. "How's your Ma n' Pa n' baby sisters doin'? I'm sure proud to know you!" As soon as they assumed I was out of earshot, however, there would be murmurs of, "That boy is so short n' pale n' skinny. Don't them parents of his feed their kids nothin'? Can't they get them some new clothes, so they don't look so ragged?"

Whenever I overheard the mockery, I would overflow with shame. Pa taught us kids that when others look down on you, keep your head high. Ma took a more active approach. If she saw my face turn groundward from hearing the harsh words of our neighbors, she would pull me aside and have me look at my reflection in her small hand mirror.

"Look at this handsome young man. Look at your bright red hair, and your deep blue eyes, and the adorable, embarrassed smile that's creepin' onto your face now.

You're shorter'n the other boys your age, but that don't matter. You ain't any less than any of the others that might have more money, and you're brighter'n all of 'em, too.

"We might not have as much money as other families around here, but you look at yourself and tell me you ain't worth somethin'. If anyone tries to come down on you, I want you to be like a rattlesnake. Make a big noise, and bite back if you have to, but don't let anyone step on you."

The attitude of defiant confidence that my mother instilled in me would define my approach to life going forward. I first got to exercise this when I insisted that I attend school beyond the single year that Pa deemed necessary. It was there that I discovered my first great love: reading.

Our schoolteacher, Ms. Appleby, adored literature and filled a bookshelf in the schoolhouse with her personal collection of favorites. She encouraged all of her students to borrow them freely. That bookshelf was as close as our town came to having a library. The instant that I worked out how to combine letters to form words, and words into sentences, I discovered a love for stories. I was especially drawn to stories of the fantastical and supernatural. Tales about mysterious creatures and ghost stories fascinated me.

In my reading I could escape from the humdrum of farming life in Shroud's Creek and travel the world. I imagined myself sailing alongside Odysseus, battling monsters and gods. The exotic, magical *Tales of 1001 Nights* mystified and enchanted me. Captain Nemo's expedition to the bottom of the ocean opened up new realms of possibilities. I came to understand that the world was so much larger and full of mystery than I could possibly imagine.

My parents disapproved of my particular taste in fiction, however. Especially my father. Every time he would see me with a book that wasn't the Farmer's Almanac, he would groan about me "wastin' my time with all that useless, stupid junk". He wasn't a mean man, just a harsh realist. If he couldn't see something with his own eyes or hold it in his hands, it wasn't worth his consideration.

It's a lot to digest at once, understanding reader, but all of these things must be understood for everything that follows to make sense. This was the setting for the event that changed my life and set the path I would follow from then onward.

The Shuck Family Farm normally turned out a modest but sufficient crop each year. During that harvesting season, however, the crops had been failing due to mysterious circumstances. The wheat and corn were dying, but not from the kind of blight that the community always watched for and took steps to prevent. This was something new and unusual.

Everyone in the town reported the same strange findings: Every morning, they would find long, winding trails of burned plants, which had been perfectly healthy the afternoon before, and *NO, I was NOT careless with the moonshine and smokes last night, thank you kindly*. The plants in its path were dead, either uprooted or singed by some unexplainable fire.

No one was spared. Every farm was hit.

Pa put forward the idea that we may have had an arsonist in town, but couldn't point anyone out as a suspect, since the fires were affecting everyone's crops (and shockingly, no one confessed). No family were more affected than us, however, and Pa was determined to prove that someone was setting fires. The next day he took me out to the wheat field so we could take a closer look.

"See here, Gunnar," he said to me, "If this were a natural fire, it would spread outward from the source. But this is goin' in a path, which means this is happ'nin' deliberately. If we look for footprints to track, we can figure out who the culprit is."

"This is kinda excitin', ain't it, Pa?" I offered.

"Excitin' in what way?" he barked back at me.

"Well, I mean... it's like a mystery. A bona-fide, honest-

to-God mystery. Like in—"
Pa interrupted, "You're about to say, 'like in one of your books,' aintcha?"
"...Well, yeah..."
"It ain't nothin' like a book. This is real. Real crops bein' damaged and real folks' livelihoods at stake, worst of all, *ours*."
I dropped the subject and went on helping my father. Using the scythe, we cut our way through the path of the dead wheat. My job was to hold and carry the inedible wheat chaff, which still had a use as kindling, if nothing else. Once a sufficient area was cleared away, we could clearly see that something had, indeed, invaded our land. To our surprise, instead of human footprints, we found a trail of two-toed hoofprints.
My father scratched his orange, scruffy beard and grumbled, "All of this don't add up."
"So... a deer is startin' the fires, Pa?" I asked innocently.
"Don't be silly. Yer old enough to know that deer can't start fires."
"What if it wasn't a deer? It coulda been a satyr."
"...a *what* now?"
"A satyr, from Greek myth. Half-man, half-goat. A thing like that would have hooves and could light a fire."
My father just stared at me in a What Am I Going to Do with That Boy kind of way, which immediately caused me to shrink. Then he stated matter-of-factly, "There ain't no such thing, and we both know it. Them book writers from foreign parts had wild imaginations, but no one's ever produced any evidence for that kinda stuff really existin'. What you gotta do when you have a real problem is come up with a real solution. Now, c'mon, son, what we're gonna do now is start building a fence, and that should keep the varmints outta the field. We should be able to get at least one side done by sundown."
Real, mythical, or otherwise, I was determined to catch the beast, in spite of what Pa said. That night, I took it upon myself to keep watch over the fields. A ten-year-

old boy will make executive decisions like that, as is their right. Pa and I had managed to finish the fence on the woods-facing side, so the others were unprotected. I took the family rifle from over the fireplace, loaded some shells, put on my boots, and stationed myself on the dark porch.

The summer heat was stifling, despite the breeze which made waves in the wheat. I scanned from left to right and back again, fighting to ignore my stinging eyes. The vacant field, illuminated by moonlight alone and the creepy silence had me on edge with anticipation. Although it was past midnight, I couldn't have fallen asleep if I wanted to.

Then, I heard it. A rustling from the field and the rhythmic *crunch crunch* of dry earth under footfalls, travelling toward me from the other side. Resting my open palm over my eyebrows (A trick every child knows extends your field of vision), I could just make out puffs of smoke rising and catching the moonlight.

'There it is!' I thought. 'That's the critter! Okay, Gunnar Shuck, time to be brave.'

I gripped my weapon tightly, which, in my shaking hands, only served to make it rattle and unsettled me further. Taking in a deep, shaky breath, I tiptoed into the field.

In my haste, I landed on a twig that snapped, and silence replaced the sounds of the creature moving. The wheat stood above my head, and with no way to see where I was going, I was operating by sound alone. Swallowing my breath and keeping perfectly still, I waited until I heard it walking again. My heart was pounding, and I took deliberate, staccato breaths.

I made a concentrated effort to place each step cautiously so that I might mitigate the crunching of the dirt. The loudest sound in the world is the one that gets you caught. This was how it went for the longest time. Movement, caution, silence, movement again, and the dance repeated.

Suddenly, erupting through the grain, I came face to face with an enormous beast that towered over me. In the dark, I could only make out the silhouette of its giant form, outlined by moonlight. It had a long, muscular neck, a face that narrowed to a pointed snout, and a pair of massive antlers branching out from its head. Its eyes glowed fiery-yellow as it glared down at me. Black smoke billowed from its nostrils.

I cowered and stared in stunned silence as its antlers suddenly burst into flame.

Illuminated by its own fire, I saw that the creature was an enormous stag rising over the wheat. Quivering, I pointed my gun at it and fired, but my shot missed, and the alarmed beast leaped over my head and ran away into the woods. As its antlers brushed the wheat, the stalks caught, and soon I was surrounded by a blazing inferno.

I ran screaming "FIRE! FIRE!" back toward the house, and soon Ma and Pa were on the porch. I heard my father curse, and then he scrambled to the washbasin to fill buckets with water. I could hear my two little sisters crying from inside the house. Pa, Ma, and I worked quickly to put out the fire, but only managed to save about half of the wheat from being consumed by the flames.

Once we had successfully stopped the blaze, Pa brought me inside and sat me down at the kitchen table. By the light of a candle, I could see that he was confused and furious. We were both covered from top to bottom with dirt and ashes.

"What in BLAZES happened, son!?" he demanded, gripping my shoulders so tightly that it hurt. "What were you doin' out so late, and with my gun?"

"I-I was tryin' to protect the farm!" I insisted. "I heard somethin' out in the field, and I went to catch it..."

"What if you got hurt? Huh? It was stupid'n reckless o' you to put yourself in danger like that! As your Pa, it's *my* job to look after the farm and my kids. Y'shoulda come and woken me up, and I woulda handled it!"

Tears boiled up in my eyes as I cried, "It WAS a deer!"

"What?"

As I described the creature I saw (making sure to add proper emphasis with wild hand gestures), the look on my father's face told me that he wasn't about to believe a word of it. Ma had finally succeeded in lulling my sisters back to sleep and entered to listen to my story, wearing a grim expression on her face. Once I had finished, I once again received that look of disapproval from Pa, which infuriated me to the point of tears, but I continued in spite of that.

"I'm not lyin'! I saw somethin' weird out there!"

My father sighed and calmly replied, "I don't think yer lyin', son, but I don't think whatcha described can be what you saw. Things like that don't exist. They just don't. It's dark out there, and it's plenty late, so maybe your imagination was playin' tricks on you."

"But... then how do you explain the fire?" I protested.

"I dunno, but it couldn't have been a... a burnin' stag. That don't make sense. Whatever it was, I want you to promise me that you'll be more careful, and never take my rifle without permission again, okay? I don't want you getting hurt."

I looked to Ma for support, but I could see from the forlorn look of total exhaustion on her face that I wouldn't receive any. Having been cornered, I agreed both to drop the topic and not put myself in harm's way.

Despite this, I knew with total conviction that I was right. I needed to learn more about the monster so that I could be better prepared when I tried to catch it again.

Chapter 2

THERE WAS ONLY ONE place in Shroud's Creek that could possibly have information I didn't already possess: the schoolhouse. So, the following morning before class, I tore through the bookshelf, hunting for anything that might lead me to the identity of the mystery creature. My search was so ferocious that there were whispers among my classmates that I'd lost my marbles.

Thankfully, they were still functionally clacking together in my skull, and when my search proved fruitless, I approached the schoolteacher, Miss Appleby. Even if she didn't take me seriously, I knew I could trust her to at least humor a curious student's inquiries.

She was a kind, grandmotherly woman, who became a teacher at the age of 17, and then went on a sixty-year lunch break to raise her own family. One day, she realized that her children had long since been raised and were now raising their own families. Her supply of kids depleted, she decided to take up teaching again. Now she was provided with a theoretically limitless rotation of grandchildren by proxy to nurture.

In simpler terms, she adored children, and relished the privilege of playing a part in their development. In her eyes, every child contained a seed of genius, and it only required the proper tending and nourishment to germinate. She was a gardener, and her harvest was a bounty of curious, thoughtful, and productive young people.

With this in mind, I felt comfortable enough to

approach Miss Appleby with my inquiries. Once the other students had left to (ostensibly) go home, I stepped up to her desk.

"Howdy, Gunnar!" she beamed with a warm smile. "Didja need—I mean—DID YOU need something explained from today's lesson? You were rippin' through the books like a twister earlier."

I embarrassedly answered, "I was trying to find some information on a critter I saw last night. Ain't never seen nothin—"

"Ah, ah, Gunnar," she sweetly interrupted. "You've forgotten yer proper grammar. Try it again."

I sighed and obediently restated, "I HAVEN'T seen ANYTHIN' like it before, and I couldn't find anythin' on it in any of the books, so I was wond'rin' if maybe you'd seen or heard about it?"

"Maybe I have. What did this animal look like?"

"It was... er..." I stammered, gazing at my shifting feet to see if I had dropped my confidence there. "Well... it's kinda hard to believe."

"Gunnar, when you've been around as long as I have, you see a lot of things that are hard to believe. Go on, tell me what you saw."

As I described the massive stag with its antlers of fire, her smile transformed into a concerned grimace that told me she had overestimated how she prepared she was to hear my outlandish story. When I got to the end, I expected to be dismissed (or committed). Instead, she tapped her fingers and pondered.

"Hmmmm..." she pondered wistfully, "I ain't never—I mean—HAVEN'T EVER heard of that or anythin' suchlike before. I'm not surprised it wasn't in any o' those books. Don't look so glum, now. There're a few more books tucked away in the broom closet. Why don't we have a look-see?"

I followed the aged educator to the front of the schoolhouse, and she opened the closet. Perusing beyond the frayed hay-bristled broom and wooden crates, we uncovered a small pile of long-neglected books. She extracted one of the ancient tomes and blew the skin of dust off of it. "Ah-ha!" she announced. "Here! Take this home with you. It might contain the answers you're lookin' for."

Its title—which could have also served as the first chapter—was *This Town: A Historical Survey of the Picturesque Farming Village of Shroud's Creek, Tennessee: from its Founding in 1800 by Zebadiah Shroud till 1850; by Surplus Cornhollister (Town Mayor, Coroner, and Barber)*.

If the contents of the book were as detailed as its title, I stood a chance of finding some useful information. I thanked her and, with the book clutched tightly under my arm, raced back to the Shuck farm so that I could study it.

I read late into the night, which normally troubled my parents, but they were relieved that I was at least reading something *factual* for a change. I skipped over the parts about the settlement of the area, genealogies, and elections (the useless stuff) and looked for major crop failures or other strange events. At last, I found an entry that shed a glimmer of light.

In a (relatively) brief chapter titled *The Blight of 1822*[1], the author described a crop failure with symptoms similar to the ones we experienced. Corn and wheat mysteriously burning with no apparent pattern. Accusations and conspiracy theories. Families leaving to find work elsewhere.

That last part proved prophetic.

What stood out most to me was that when the man who was accused of starting the fires was caught—a "vagrant" named Bobby Brewer—he was questioned and came up with a "preposterous" story about a beast with "horns of fire" that was the true cause. He called it the "Not-Deer".

---

[1] Actually, the full chapter title was *The Blight of 1822, in which an Inexplicable Series of Burnings Led to a Major Crop Failure, Culminating in the Subsequent Apprehension of One Robert Brewer, and the Absurd Alibi the Accused put Forth to Avoid Conviction*, but I thought it would be best not to waste the kind reader's time with this.

His exact words were, "Well, 'twere a deer, and at the same time, 'tweren't a deer. 'Twere made o' fire. What kinda critter's made o' fire? Not deer. Any way a fella could get a drink in here?" No suitable replacement for the uncreative name was ever conceived of, so it's known as a "not-deer" by Tennesseans to this day.

This was proof enough to me that what I had seen was real, but it was a warning that I ought to keep it to myself. Telling the open-minded Miss Appleby about it was one thing, but most folks would draw the conclusion that I had gone loony, and that wouldn't do any good for anyone. Why, I doubt any of them would believe their own eyes if the Not-Deer trotted right up and blew smoke in their faces.

I didn't give up on my search for the creature, however. In fact, it strengthened my resolve that I, and I alone should be the one to stop it.

With my determination fortified, I considered potential strategies for my second attempt to capture my nemesis. Would I stand guard like I had the first night? It was detrimental to my sleep, and the results were far from ideal.

Perhaps there was a way to trap the creature? How would I ensnare a stag made of fire? No one, to my knowledge, had ever attempted it before. Ordinary trapping methods would not suffice, since the Not-Deer could simply burn its way through a net or snare. No, I would have to be creative.

Water, I reasonably supposed, would be a vital element in the construction of my traps. If the creature could be doused, perhaps it could be more easily subdued. It was also a precious resource that Summer, and hardly a drop could be spared for anything frivolous.

But this couldn't be considered frivolous, could it? Surely a touch of dehydration was a worthy sacrifice to put an end to the burnings. Everyone was bound to see it that way when I had a pair of smoky antlers to hang on the wall.

I set about designing a water-themed trap. Even though the field was irrigated, the thirsty earth and roots quickly absorbed any moisture spread to them. I needed to keep the water from being sucked up by the ground or drying up in the hot Tennessee sun. So, I collected every bucket, basin, and tin cup I could get my hands on, and placed them beneath the stalks of corn and wheat.

Then, I waited.

Admittedly, it wasn't the most complex of designs, but I wouldn't have to wait long to get results. The following afternoon, while my sisters and I were collecting eggs from the chicken coop, we heard a commotion from the field. A noisome splash, followed by a shriek, and then squelching, muddy stomps approaching us. Something had stumbled into my trap!

"Pa!" I called with excitement. "It worked! My trap worked!"

I was instantly proved a fool for celebrating as, to my horror, what emerged from the field was my father, dripping wet, with a bucket stuck on each foot. His face was as red from rage as mine was becoming from embarrassment, and if he could frown any more his jaw would separate from his head.

Ellie snickered at the ridiculous sight of Pa and the anticipation of the trouble her brother was in. Rosie poked out her tongue and giggled. The furious anger on Pa's face froze me to the spot, mortifying me more than even the Not-Deer had.

"DAGNABBIT, GUNNAR!" Pa erupted. "So, this is *yer* trap, huh? Are ya lookin' to catch a whuppin? What got into yer head to do a bone-headed thing like this!?"

"It—I—Um..." I stammered, unable to generate any kind of excuse that would satisfy my red-faced, raging father.

I didn't catch a whupping, for despite using it as a threat, my father never actually struck any of his children. However, I did earn a month's worth of mucking out the cow pen and chicken coop. After that fracas, I silently decided that I would never set another trap. I would simply keep vigil, watch for the creature, and make my move when I saw it.

Every day while I worked alongside my father in the fields and barn, I kept a sharp eye for signs. A burnt stick, a set of hoofprints, any evidence of the Not-Deer's having been there. Every night I fell asleep listening for the sound of the beast's footsteps and watching for the flames.

Although my watch was unyielding, I never saw the Not-Deer again. Perhaps it had become more cautious after nearly being shot that night and decided not to forage on our property a second time. Despite its never reappearing at the Shuck farm, the burnings continued everywhere else in the town.

Years passed and the century turned, and the crops continued to be blighted by the elusive, fiery menace. People took notice that ours was the only farm that no longer suffered from fires, and before long, we found ourselves totally friendless. Accusations and anger boiled in the community, escalating more and more, until no family would associate with another, least of all the dirt poor, suspicious Shucks.

It's not as though we were any better off than they were. Even though our crops were no longer burning, my family was forced to make many sacrifices to make ends meet. Since we were thoroughly detested in town, the crops we were able to reap were sold well below market price, and we had to accept it out of desperation.

Every week, another item of furniture would mysteriously disappear, and if any of us children asked about it, we were only offered the irritated answer of, "*Never mind what happened to the rockin' chair. Ain't it better to have food on the table?*"

This answer ceased to placate us once the table vanished. Along with our chairs and table, my parents had sold the cabinets and all but one bed. I had to share that with my sisters, an especially cramped arrangement for me since my legs hung over the side. My parents slept on a pile of blankets next to the fireplace. Sometimes, if his back ached too much to sit on the floor, Pa would drag the chopping block in from outside to sit on.

At the same time, the second decade of my life was underway, and my body began expanding to accommodate puberty. My clothes, however, could not do the same, so my shirtsleeves and pant legs quickly retreated up my arms and legs. I brought my concerns for my wardrobe and decency to ma, saying that a purchase of new clothes may be necessary.

Her response was to tear a fragment off of the drapery and sew it on to my clothes.

"There," she grumbled. "Now it's like you've got a brand-new shirt."

For the next few years, all of our clothes had to be patched or modified in this manner whenever they were torn, or we grew out of them. Soon my shirt sleeves had several rings of cloth where they had been lengthened to keep up with my arms, my pant legs only came down to my shins, and my toes stuck out from the fronts of the boots I had outgrown.

Finally, in the Summer of 1901, when I turned fourteen, my family could withstand no more, and we were forced to make the difficult decision to leave. At that time, each of us felt like it was the end of the world.

Soon, however, it would prove to be the beginning of a new one.

Chapter 3

My father was a stubborn man when it came to asking for help. If he was trapped under, say, a runaway wagon, he would sooner cut off his own leg to free himself than ask someone else to roll it off of him. He would say he didn't want to owe anything to anyone. At the same time, he wouldn't hesitate to lend a hand to anyone else who asked him. No one likes to point out the hypocrisy of this for fear of seeming ungrateful.

This is why it was astonishing to me when I found him late one night resorting to a desperate measure he never took, at least never in front of his children.

He composed a letter.

That night I was awoken by the sound of my parents angrily whispering to one another, and my father's heavy footsteps pacing around the house. Pa never stirred in the middle of the night. He always fell asleep at precisely 9:17 in the evening and awoke at 5:29 at the first rooster's crow to start work.

I knew then that something must be wrong and decided to spy on them to see what was going on.

Hidden by shadows, I peeked around the corner from my bedroom to the kitchen of our house. My father was sitting directly on the floor (the attentive reader will remember we sold all of our chairs and tables), a stack of blank pages spread out in front of him next to a pen and dusty inkwell. He hung there stewing in his guilt and self-anger illuminated by dim candlelight.

Ma stood behind him, hand on his shoulder, her face as solemn as his.

"I know how much you hate to ask for help," she whispered, "but it's the only way to save our family."

He grumbled in response, "I don't even know if she'll answer me. We ain't talked in a long time..."

"Luke, she's your aunt. You told me that before she left, she said you could write her a letter any time. Remember that? I think it's your stubborn pride that's kept you from it for so long, but now we're desperate, and need you to be strong."

Pa cast his gaze down at the floor and rubbed his temples, a sign that he would rather be doing anything than having this conversation. Not one to be shut out by anyone, least of all her own husband, Ma placed her hand on his chin and brought his eyes back up to hers.

"Don't you turn away from me when I'm talkin to you, darlin'," she said sternly.

"...Yes, Mary..." he whimpered.

"Now I know you're gonna do the right thing, hun. We both know we can't go on livin' here anymore. I haven't told the kids but if things keep up like this, we won't be able to feed ourselves this Winter. It won't be easy, but you gotta ask your aunt to help you find work and a place to live in Pennsylvania. Don't let us down."

Worse than making someone angry is disappointing them. A person can come up with any excuse why someone shouldn't be mad at them, but when they are disappointed, that's on *you*.

Ma left him to turn in for the night, and after she closed their bedroom door, my father knew there would be no getting out of it. Either he went through with writing his letter, or he'd have to explain to an angry wife why he hadn't. He contemplated alone for a long time; head supported on two index fingers while he composed drafts in his mind.

Finally, he lifted his pen, dipped it in the inkwell, and began to write. The expression on his face betrayed how much he hated himself for what he was doing. Overcome with emotion, he growled, crumpled up the page and threw it across the kitchen. He took a fresh page and attempted once more to compose his letter, but the same frustration got the better of him.

This went on until a pile of paper balls formed in the corner of the room.

He had to take some time to compose himself, sighed deeply, and took up the pen and a fresh sheet of paper once more. This time, through heavy breaths and patience, he was able to write the letter that said what he needed to. At the end, he folded the note, slid it into an envelope, addressed it, and sealed it with a bit of wax dripped from his candle. He guiltily added it to his pile of things to bring with him when he drove into town in the morning.

I had never, nor have I ever since seen my father so defeated.

Two weeks later, Pa sat everyone down at breakfast to make an announcement. He held an opened letter in his hand. He was trying to appear confident, but the wrinkling of his eyebrows told me that he was in truth, seriously nervous. He only wore that expression when he had a major decision to make and expected that no matter what, everyone would be displeased with him.

"Look here, kids. Two weeks ago, I wrote a letter to my Aunt Shannon in Pennsylvania. Now, I ain't heard from her in, oh... many years. When I was still a boy she got married to a rich merchant from the north, and she moved there with him. I wrote her a few weeks back because, honestly... *sigh*... things ain't goin' so good for us here. I had to ask her for some help. Now I'm gonna share with you what she wrote here."

"Ooh, how excitin'!" Ma said obligatorily, trying to prime us kids to be receptive to what the letter might say. This did little to calm my sisters' apprehension about this unusual letter. They looked nervously between each parent and myself, looking for some guidance on how to feel.

Pa ceremoniously opened it, held it up at arm's length as if it smelled like rotten onions, and read:

"Dearest Luke,

I am all too pleased to hear from you again after such a long time, although the... [Pa paused to sound out the next word] *cir-cum-stances you described for you and your family distressed me greatly. Long ago I gave you my word that I would be there to lend assistance if ever you asked for it, and now I'm goin' to make good on that promise.*

There is a carpentry shop here in the town of Raspberry Hill, and I have spoken with the manager. He was most... en-thu-si-astic that he should hire on a man skilled in craftsmanship, such as I'm certain you are.

Additionally, since I have no children of my own and my dear husband has been dead these past seven years, I am all alone in my home here, save for the nurse and doctor who pay me a daily visit. I would be delighted if you and your family would move into the house to live with me and keep me company.

When you arrive in town, stop by the office of Hammeboerger and Freiss, my estate lawyers. They will provide you with house keys.

With much love and... an-ti-ci-pating our reunion,
Your Aunt Shannon Hollinger"

Pa lowered the letter, bracing himself for our reactions. Ma smiled at each of us, a subtle hint that we should respond with similar enthusiasm. There were some protests from my wide-eyed and furrow-browed sisters, however.

"What about the farm, Pa?" asked Ellie, now nine years old. "We still have a few chickens, the horse, and about half a field o' wheat."

Pa calmly answered, "It ain't enough to sustain us here. You kids are sharin' a bed and growin' as fast as y'are that ain't gonna work for long. Our clothes are in tatters, and we can barely put food on the table. We've tried as hard as we can, but this year we didn't earn enough to make us through Winter. We can't stay here livin' in poverty no more. So tomorrow mornin' we're gonna sell the animals and the farm for what we can get, and then we're gonna buy train tickets and head out to Raspberry Hill."

"I'm unna missa chickies..." complained five-year-old Rosie.

"I don't mind wearin' hand-me-downs, Pa. Plus I don't want to leave my friends!" protested Ellie.

"That's enough, girls," scolded Ma. "Pa and I have made up our minds and we're going to do what's best."

"Say somethin', Gunnar!" Ellie prompted me. "You have friends here, and you love the farm as much as anybody! Tell them we can't leave!"

Pa must have expected that I would hold the same attitude as my sisters, since he gave me a sideways glance. However, I knew how hard it was for him to make this decision to give up the family farm and everything we knew. After being beaten down by circumstance for the past few years, and indeed, the whole of his life, I recognized that now he needed my support.

"I think Pa's makin' a wise choice," I replied, surprising everyone. "We can't go on here anymore, and this gives us an opportunity to start fresh and make things better."

Ma was pleased to hear me say that, and I suppose Pa was too, although he cast his eyes down at the floor, apparently ashamed that he had expected the worst from me. Realizing that they were outnumbered, my sisters caved and agreed to not argue any more, albeit begrudgingly.

The following morning, we hitched the horse up to our wagon and loaded up everything we could fit. Pa took a minute to say goodbye to the old place, a rare display of sentimentality from him. I understood though, as it was the place where he and countless ancestors were born, raised, lived, and died.

    I stood beside him during those moments of silent reflection, but my attention was divided. My eyes kept turning to the fields where I had my strange encounter with the not-deer. Before we rode out, I swear I saw its silhouette one more time. It did not seem to notice me.

Chapter 4

AFTER SELLING THE FARM, the animals, and even the wagon in town, we purchased train tickets and for the first time in a while, new clothes. Ma said that we should look presentable and not so haggard when we arrived in Raspberry Hill.

For the first time in my life, I was permitted to choose my own wardrobe. I thought I looked quite handsome in the form-fitting overalls, shirt, and vest I selected for myself.

Ma tried on a selection of different dresses, and each one she tried inspired my sisters to hunt for ones that matched. They settled on a trio of white dresses with coral trim, with a sun hat for Ma. Pa's only requirement for his clothes was that they fit and have no other holes than spacious pockets.

Afterward, a coach was hired to take us to the train station. It was really just a platform a mile out of town. If the passing engineers poked their heads out and didn't see anyone, they wouldn't even stop. The tracks and the earthy brick platform were the only signs of civilization around, and the train nearly passed us by before they noticed there were people standing there waiting to be picked up.

We boarded and were carried to Nashville, where we made our connecting train to Harrisburg, Pennsylvania. On that magnificent locomotive, the somber mood turned around entirely. Suddenly we forgot about everything we were leaving behind, and it became a wondrous adventure.

The Appalachian Mountains loomed over us as the train travelled alongside them. My sisters and I—who had never previously travelled outside of Shroud's Creek—were amazed at the hugeness of them. I had read stories about daring journeys through mountain ranges but seeing them in person was so much more impressive.

After reaching Harrisburg and making one more connection on a local train, we finally reached Raspberry Hill. My first impression of the town was how much smaller it seemed than Shroud's Creek, even though I could see that there were far more houses. In fact, this is what seemed strange about it to me, that I *could* see the entire town as soon as I stepped off the train.

We were greeted by the chiming of bells, sourced from the Gothic church at the far end of town, informing all its residents that noontime had arrived. Its steeple stabbed up at the sky, above even the woods and mountains that loomed behind it.

The sound travelled along Main Street, which wound its way in a broad S-curve from the church all the way to its terminus at the train station. On either side of this road were the many shops, restaurants, and offices of the town. Beyond them were the many houses the townsfolk lived in.

Walking up the hill, we arrived at the law office of Hammeboerger and Freiss. We were greeted inside by the lawyers themselves. John Hammeboerger, a round gentleman with a bushy moustache and a well-rehearsed smile, welcomed us in. His associate Frederick Freiss, a wiry bald fellow that reminded me of a walking stick bug, sat at a desk reading the newspaper.

The theme of the office was brown. Brown wooden cabinets sat on either side of the walnut desks on the hardwood floor. Even the suits the lawyers wore were brown tweed. Hammeboerger, puffing on his brown pipe, invited us to sit down in the brown chairs across from him

at the desk. The wood groaned under the weight of people moving around and wailed when chairs scraped across it.
"What can I help you fine folks with this afternoon?" the portly lawyer asked.
My father said, "I'm Luke Shuck, this is my wife, Mary, and these are our children."
"Please to meet you sir, ma'am," the lawyer replied, showing off the most impressive toothy smile he could muster. "And what handsome children you have. Aren't they, Mr. Freiss?"
Without looking up from his paper, the other lawyer replied in a nasally monotone, "Truly a credit to good breeding, Mr. Hammeboerger."
"Well put, Frederick. I'm sure I have some sweets around here somewhere. Would you like sweets, children?" We didn't need any after the saccharine we had just been force-fed, but the lawyer didn't wait for a response before rummaging through his desk drawers. Before long, he fruitlessly admitted, "It appears I'm all out. I could have sworn I had caramels. Anyway, what can I do for you folks today?"
Pa answered, "We just arrived off the train from Tennessee and came straight here like we were told to. So… here we are."
Hammeboerger's smile didn't leave his face, but he paused in momentary confusion. "Here you are, indeed…?"
My father looked around the room, himself now lost, and said, "You weren't expectin' us?"
At this, the lawyer turned to his partner, teeth still showing, and asked, "Mr. Freiss, were we expecting Mr. and Mrs. Shuck today?"
The man didn't look up from his paper, but drily responded, "The name sounds familiar, but we don't have an appointment with any Shucks that I know of."
"I'm Shannon Hollinger's nephew," my father explained. "I understand that y'all are my aunt's estate lawyers?"

Recognition flooded John's eyes. "That's where I've heard your name before! Yes, indeed. We've been trying to reach you, but we didn't know how to contact you."

"Aunt Shannon didn't leave you an address?" Ma asked with a raised eyebrow.

Hammeboerger noticed the eyebrow and proceeded carefully. "No, ma'am. No address. Just the name of the town, Shroud's Creek, Tennessee. Not enough to go by, you understand."

"And what stopped you from reachin' out to the town council to ask after the whereabouts of one of its citizens?"

The two lawyers gave sidelong, conspiratorial glances to one another, before Freiss finally answered, "By Jove, you're right, madam. It completely escaped us."

"We really should have considered that," John snakily conceded before tactfully shifting the subject, "But it's a good thing you came today, as a matter of fact. We have a lot to go over with you."

I could see from the twitching of Ma's eye muscles that they were straining to resist the urge to roll.

Pa replied, "Well, we came as soon as we could from down South. Is my Aunt here now?"

Hammeboerger's demeanor sobered. Freiss looked up from his newspaper with curiosity.

"She... well... No, she isn't..."

"Maybe we could reach her by the telephone? Or call on her at her house?"

"You don't know, Mr. Shuck?" My father remained silent, merely shrugging his shoulders. John continued, "Oh dear... I'm sorry to be the one to inform you of this, but your aunt has passed on."

I could see from the look in Pa's eyes that his heart sunk down into the pit of his gut and spilled onto the floor upon receiving that news, and it took him a few moments to collect himself before he could respond.

"Goodness gracious... and we just got a letter from her last week. This is... unexpected."

The lawyers looked at each other with concern, then Freiss said, "Mr. Shuck, Shannon Hollinger died six months ago."

This shocked all of us, even little Rosie who possessed a basic grasp of linear time.

"Six months? But I just received a letter from her this week. I have it here."

Pa reached into his coat pocket, removed the folded letter, and handed it to the lawyer. Hammeboerger pulled out a pair of reading glasses (brown, naturally), placed them on his nose and began to examine the letter. Freiss stood up from his desk and crept over so that he could inspect it, too, nearly touching noses with his associate.

"This is her handwriting, to be sure," pondered Hammeboerger.

Freiss added, "Indeed, the letter is authentic. Maybe it got lost in the post for a while? That can happen sometimes."

"But this is a response to a letter I wrote her only three weeks ago!"

"Look at the postmark, John," Freiss said, jabbing at the envelope. "That's last Tuesday's date. The post office really did send this out last week. What could that mean?"

At this point, I had formulated some theories of my own. My first thought was that the letter may have been written by her ghost or some sort of changeling, but I had the good sense not to bring that up in the present company. Hammeboerger didn't have any kind of explanation to offer, so he changed the subject.

"What does it matter when the letter was sent out? You're here now, and just in the nick of time, as it happens. Like I said, we've been trying to find you since Mrs. Hollinger passed because she left her entire estate to you in her will. If you had arrived even a day later, the bank would have claimed all of the assets that are rightfully yours."

"Her *entire* estate?" Ma gasped. "What all does that entail?"

Freiss answered, "It includes her house with all furnishings and assets therein, as well as the funds in her bank account, save for the donations she made to various charitable organizations before her passing, and of course, our legal fees for this transaction."

"Of course..." Pa and Ma said in unison.

"Here," Friess said, sauntering to a filing cabinet, which he unlocked, thumbed through its contents, and produced a ledger. He opened it to a particular page and handed it to parents, pointing and explaining, "Here you can see the total value of the estate, which you will control."

When Ma and Pa took a look at the sum at the bottom of the page, both of their jaws came crashing down on the floor. It was apparently more money than they had ever known existed.

"Holy smokes!" exclaimed Pa.

"We wich now?" Rosie asked innocently.

My parents shushed her, but John chuckled and answered, "Certainly you'll be very comfortable. It's a marvelous house. Frederick, you have the keys in your safe, is that right?"

"That's right, Mr. Hammeboerger."

"Excellent! Fetch those for the Shucks while I call up a carriage. I wish I could take you myself, but we're very busy here, I'm sure you understand. Oh, and while we wait for that, I'm going to need you to sign a few things..."

Chapter 5

THE CARRIAGE RIDE TO the house allowed us to see Main Street up close. Raspberry Hill was an old town, with an atmosphere that could best be described as "colonial." The antique wooden storefronts and offices made one feel as if they had been transported back in time to an era when American independence was still a controversial topic.

There were a wide variety of shops and offices, at least relative to the severely limited Shroud's Creek. I was amazed to see both a general store *and* a food market, and not in the same building, but separate businesses! The coexistence of a post office, bank, and courthouse made me wonder why they also had a town hall, and what was possibly left for them to do there.

Across from town hall, I was delighted to find that this town had a bona-fide library which I was eager to take advantage of. Finally, I could expand my literary repertoire beyond the handful of books that were previously available to me (although in all honesty, I was more likely to revisit my favorites.)

Pa spotted the carpentry shop and asked the driver to stop so he could run inside and speak to the manager.

"Wait," Ma protested as he climbed out of the carriage. "You saw how much money we're inheritin'. Why d'you wanna work still?"

Pa considered this and answered, "Well, dear, my thinkin' goes like this: We got that money by pure luck, not because I did anything to earn it. So maybe by workin' I can eventually feel like I *did* earn it. Besides, you know me, sweetheart. I can't just sit around idle. These hands need to work to stay happy."

He entered the shop, and mere minutes later, returned with a beaming smile on his face.

"Looks like it went well," Ma said.

"Oh, it sure did! I met the owner, Mr. Llanfair. Swell fella; seems like he'll be a good boss. I introduced myself and asked for the job, and he said, 'That's the least I can do to honor the memory of Shannon Hollinger. A man with your experience should be workin' as a foreman, and I want to offer you the position.'"

"So, you're gonna be managing the team here?" Ma replied excitedly.

"No! I said to him, 'No sir, I'm not here to tell other people what to do. I'm a workin' man, and a craftsman, so I'll be woodworkin', or I won't be workin' at all.' Well, my cunnin' words persuaded 'im, so I'll be startin' as a lathe operator."

"Oh..." Ma deflated.

"I understand yer disappointment, hun. I was hopin' I'd be workin' straightaway, too. I even offered to start tomorrow, but Llanfair said I ought to take a few days to settle in. We compromised and I agreed to take tomorrow off and start the day after. Hear that, kids?"

Pa's expectant gaze passed over each of us. I faked a smile as best I could. Ellie was wide-eyed in confusion. Little Rosie didn't really comprehend any of it.

Pa reiterated, "Didncha hear what I said? Yer old man has 'imself a job again!"

The only one of us who missed that Pa had made a silly mistake was Rosie, who hopped up and down with a "Yay, Papa!"

Ellie, Ma, and I collectively groaned. Oh well, with the inheritance, we wouldn't actually have to worry about money anymore. At least Pa was happy, even if ignorantly so.

The coach rode onward up the hill. Before we made the turn onto the street our house was on, an unusual shop caught my eye, and time seemed to slow down as I took it all in.

The hanging sign over the doorframe read **L. Mortenson's Curiosities, Unusual Sundries, and Medium Services.**

The store front was earth-red brick, as opposed to the wooden siding of the other stores. It seemed even older than they were, the bricks cracking and dusty, with black dirt staining the mortar. The window glass was warped from centuries of gravity's influence. It was as if the store itself was an antique.

In my state of heightened awareness, I could make out all sorts of odd items in the shop display through the front windows. There were baubles with feathers and beads, bottles of colorful fluids, and objects I couldn't have even begun to describe, they were so alien to me at the time.

While examining a pair of moon-yellow beads through the distorted glass, I was surprised to see them blinking at me. I realized that I was staring into a pair of gleaming, slit-pupiled eyes. They gazed piercingly at me and almost as soon as I realized I was being watched, they turned away and a small, midnight-black body retreated into the store.

A poster in another window read,

Are you Afflicted by Unexplained Occurrences?

Are you Haunted or been Visited by Spirits from beyond the grave?

Has a Strange Creature taken up Residence in your home?

If so, please come speak to Mr. Levi Mortenson, professional Medium, Paranormal Researcher, and seller of Curious Artifacts.

Open Weekdays and all holidays Except Hallowe'en and Christmas.

How could I not be intrigued by this? I had previously only encountered the supernatural as stories in books, and the single encounter I had with the not-deer. No one had believed it was real, and I was even starting to dismiss that night as only a child's dream. But here was a shop dedicated to the paranormal. It gave my experience firm grounding, and for the first time, I felt validated.

This feeling was shortly snuffed out however, and my father was its assassin.

Pa's reaction was the perfect opposite of mine. "Ugh, d'you see that?" he sneered. "That's what happens when you fill up yer head with horse hockey. You either become a crazy quack sellin' snake oil, or one of the fools they dupe into buyin' it. I don't want you goin' in there, son."

"I won't, Pa," I lied.

Of course, I was going to check out the store the first opportunity I got. What was my father going to do, watch my every move all day? I was a fourteen-year-old boy (practically a man as far as I was concerned) and I could go wherever I pleased, with or without my father's approval. Naturally, I'd keep it a secret where I'd been when I came back to his house afterward.

The carriage turned onto our street, and as our distance from the main street increased, so did the size of the houses. Every house we passed was grander than the last.

Finally, we stopped at the last, and largest, house on the street, a towering, dark, oaken mansion with an iron spoked fence running around the perimeter. The imposing architecture seemed to hang over anyone standing under it. It was both impressive and intimidating.

This house looked big enough for the entire population of Shroud's Creek to live in, and it was all ours? The idea baffled the imagination.

"Well, here we are. The old Hollinger Manor," said the coachman, removing his hat as if he were standing on the grounds of some kind of holy temple. Even his horse nickered out of respect. He helped Pa unload our bags from the carriage roof before driving away, leaving us standing in the shadow of our new home.

All any of us could do for a minute was stare straight up at the towering spires and innumerable windows that decorated the outside of the house. Wide-eyed and frozen to the spot, the only noise to be heard was the wind singing in the mountain forest to the north.

Ma was the first to break the silence. "Let's not waste any more time," she said. "It's just a house. *Our* house, now. There's nothin' to be afraid of..." Ma looked over to her daunted husband, gave him an encouraging shove from behind, and added, "Luke, you go in first."

Pa stepped cautiously onto the porch, as if it might explode beneath him. Indeed, his first footfall produced such a monstrous creak from the old wood that he leapt backward onto the gravel.

"Oh, stop foolin' around and open the door," Ma scolded.

"Tarnations, Mary! This house has a presence to it. One you don't want to upset by gettin' too familiar too quick."

"Are you superstitious, Pa?" I goaded. "I thought you said that and suchlike was horse hockey."

"Dadgummit, if everyone could just calm their goats and be patient!"

He made a second, braver advance on the front doors which—like a pair of bronze palace guards—stood twice as high as him. He removed the iron key Freiss had given him from his coat pocket, inserted it into the keyhole on the right door, and turned it.

There was a loud clanking as the doors unlocked and swung open.

Chapter 6

STEPPING INTO THE ENTRYWAY of our new home, we were greeted by an overpowering aroma of oldness. This was most gracious of it since it had been living here far longer than anyone else ever had. It was not a bad smell, just the sort that takes up residence, has a family, then demands a place at the table in recompense for the many years of service it has rendered.

This was the scent of centuries; of an old home that had seen generations come and go. It hung in the air of the murkily lit foyer as if to say, "Oh, moving in, are we? Fine, I suppose I can make room, but my discontent will be known."

Soft light lazily glistened from frosted windows high on the walls. A mountainous staircase was the centerpiece of the room, with an elaborately decorated brass chandelier hanging over it. It was additionally ornamented by cobwebs that had accumulated from months of neglect.

On the back wall, at the top of the first flight of stairs, was an enormous portrait of the mansion's last occupant and our late benefactor. For the first time, I saw the visage of the mysterious great-aunt Shannon.

She was a tall woman, at least that was the impression rendered on the massive canvas, wearing a goldenrod silk sundress and seated in a garden. Even among the violets, tulips, and roses, she stood out more radiantly. Her neck was adorned with a strawberry-sized sapphire on a gold chain. On top of her head was a wide-brimmed sunhat, topped with lace and a bouquet of pink and purple peonies.

She was seated in a wicker armchair, the woven twine lovingly detailed, frays and all. In contrast to the impressive dress, jewelry, and flowers she was surrounded by, this chair seemed modest and homely. Perhaps it was something she treasured that held a deep personal significance.

I then focused on the face of my great-aunt. Even past the wrinkles and crow's feet—which the artist had done his best to minimize but had been included nonetheless, possibly at her own insistence—the viewer could plainly see that in life, she had been a strikingly beautiful woman. Her pale blonde hair still contained some of the flame-red that ran in our family. The subtle curve of her smile was undercut by the gaze of her frosty-blue eyes, which betrayed an underlying sadness.

The markers of age on her face told me that this was a fairly recent portrait. Also, the artist had helpfully placed the date "1898" in the corner next to their signature, which was another good clue.

I caught my father gazing sadly at this painting. Screwing up his face was all he could do to fight back the swarm of emotions that assaulted him. He noticed my noticing him, and swiftly swallowed his feelings lest they should be revealed to his son.

"Er, ah-hem," he coughed. "Last time I saw 'er, she was still a young woman, drivin' away in a coach with her new fiancée, and I was a bull-headed young boy. Felt so betrayed that she left the family to marry that rich northern merchant that I *let that* be the last time."

Before I could offer any words of consolation to reply with, he terminated the subject by clapping his hands and announcing, "Well, nothin' can be done about that now. Whatcha think of our new home, girls?"

"What kinda room is this?" asked Ellie. "There are no beds, or a pantry, or nothin', just a big staircase!"

"It's called a foy-yay," answered Ma.

"What's it for?"

"If I understand rich folk architecture correctly, the point is to intimidate people."

"It's sure doin' that..." muttered Pa.

"Big house! ...house! ...house!" Rosie called out, giggling when her voice echoed back to her.

"It's more than a house, Rosie. It's called a manor," I contributed. "That's one of the differences between poor and rich folks. Poor folks have houses, and rich folks have manors."

"Manners? ...Manners? ...Manners?" my baby sister parroted along.

"I call it too good to be true," Pa said pessimistically. "There's got to be a catch in this somewhere."

My sisters and I ran up the stairs to start exploring, and I excitedly called back, "Well, we're gonna take a look around, and I'll letcha know if I find one!"

The following period of exploration played out as we called across the house to report our discoveries.

"This kitchen is huge! It even has an icebox to keep our food cold. It's so fancy and modern! There's all sorts of china and silverware in here, too."

"Is there a table to eat on with all o' them fancy-pants dishes?"

"...Yes hun, but it ain't in the kitchen. It's in the dinin' room."

"Hold yer horses. We have one room for preparin' food and another entire separate room for eatin' it?"

"Yes, and where are you anyway, Luke? You should see this."

"I'm in the cellar, cleanin' cobwebs."

"What're you doin' that for? We might have enough money now to pay someone else to clean the house!"

"Why would I pay someone else to do a job that I can do myself?"

"You're gonna have to change your thinkin' a little now that we're rich."

"That ain't a good reason to not still be smart, too.

Maybe it's a good enough excuse fer some, but not me."

"Ma, Pa, you have to come upstairs and see this! There're enough bedrooms for us each to have our own, and *then* some!"

"That's incredible, Gunnar! Looks like you won't have to share with your sisters anymore."

"Wonder if there's a way to sell extra rooms that you ain't got a use for..."

Suddenly Ellie shrieked, "EEK! THIS HOUSE HAS SOME KINDA TORTURE CHAMBER UP HERE!"

This warranted group investigation. Everyone rushed to the room where my sister had cried out from, expecting (and in my case, secretly hoping) to find something horrible and gruesome. Instead, we came together in a small room with a porcelain bowl filled with water and a pull chain hanging over it.

"See!?" she cried, urgently pointing to the fixture. "It's like somethin' outta the 'mid-evil' period. They must've used it to make people confess by dunkin' their head in the water, and if they refused, they'd pull the chain to make 'em think they were drownin'! Ain't that just awful?"

Ma closed her hand over her mouth to hold back laughter, and I felt quite let down, but Pa was simply relieved.

"Er... sweetie," he pointed out, placing a grounded paternal hand on her head. "That ain't no instrument o' torture. It's the commode."

"This is just the washroom, Ellie..." I realized, too disappointed to find amusement in my sister's foible.

Ellie was confused at our confusion. She mumbled, "Yeah, but... shouldn't that be outside? What's it doin' in the house?"

"Indoor plumbin'," Ma explained while fighting the urge to snicker. "I guess it's just another thing we're gonna have to get used to."

After the excitement, each of us kids chose a bedroom. The door at the end of the west wing spoke to me, so to speak, and appealed to my secluded adolescent spirit. No longer would I have to share a bed, a room, or even a hemisphere of the building with my sisters. For the first time in my life, I could close a door and be alone in the privacy of a small universe that was all my own.

So, I did just that, and took in the strange new sensation of solitude.

Chapter 7

My room wasn't particularly large, but after sharing a single bed with two sisters, it felt like an entire mansion in and of itself. A single window illuminated the room, and dust floated through the light that landed on the wooden floor. The wallpaper had a pattern of thorns and blackbirds, and there was another door with a small closet inside.

The room was already fully furnished with a single bed, a wardrobe, and a writing desk, upon which sat a candleholder and matchbook. I sat down on the edge of my bed and gave it an inaugural bounce to test its comfiness. The springs creaked slightly as I did so. Next, I spun around to lay down and to my amazement, my legs didn't hang over the edge. It almost didn't feel right.

I stood and went to inspect the closet. Inside I found a row of shirts, trousers, and vests. At first I expected that they had been forgotten by the previous occupant, but then I held one or two articles against my body, and puzzlingly, I found that they were a perfect fit for me. It was as if they had been tailor-made in anticipation of my arrival. Aunt Shannon didn't have any children, so why, I wondered, was this closet full of clothes that fit me exactly?

I considered this alongside the timing of Shannon's death and subsequent letter, and shuddered to think that my earlier theory about ghosts might have some validity.

While I was pondering this mystery, I was given quite a shock when part of the wall shifted, and I heard something like a frightened gasp. I replied with a matching inhalation and before I could get a look at what made the wall move, I heard it scamper away behind it.

Examining the loose panel of the wall with my fingernails, I found that I could pull it away to reveal a small doorway just large enough for me to crouch through. I slid it open and peeked my head through the hole.

A secret passage!

There was a narrow hallway that extended into darkness. The sound of tiny paws retreated into the shadows, accompanied by, it seemed, a faint whimpering. This house hadn't been lived in for months, so I wasn't surprised that critters would have moved in and settled down here.

I decided I'd worry about evicting them later. My curiosity had me by the reigns, and I needed to explore the passage.

I grabbed the candle on my writing desk and lit it, taking my first intrepid steps crabwise into the hole. The floor was padded by old fragments of rug, so I could steal through noiselessly.

I must have passed by my sisters' rooms, because I could faintly hear Ellie through the wall, saying to herself, "*...and the wardrobe should be moved to* this *side of the room, so I can put a doll shelf here, and... ooh! I'll see if Pa will let me paint it yellow...*"

Further down I heard the rhythmic squeaking of Rosie jumping up and down on her bed and singing, "*Princess Rosie, la, la-la! Princess Rosie, la, la-laaaa!*"

Shuffling in the darkness, I came upon a ladder that led down to the ground floor. I carefully lowered myself to the bottom, awkwardly holding the candlestick between my teeth so I would have both hands to grip the ladder with.

Once safely on the ground, I hit a crossroads, so to speak, as the path split into left and right passageways. Since I didn't have a coin to flip, I decided to explore the left side first, reasoning that since we read from left to right, it was as good a place to start as any.

The end of this cramped passage opened into a seclusive little chamber, windowless and dark, with a small table in its center and a single chair beside it. On the table was a circle of strange runes and symbols, written in chalk, and a ring of brass candlesticks dripping with red wax frozen midway in its journey to the floor.

At the center of this bizarre altar was a brass stand holding up a glass orb, or rather, what used to be one, for it had split several ways into chunks and shards. Based on the stories that I had read I reasoned that it must be a crystal ball, used by soothsayers and fortune tellers to see into the future.

This was certainly a shocking find. Was my great aunt involved in the occult? What was she trying to see into the future for? The only thing I could assume with any confidence was *where* she could have gotten it all from. There was only one place in town I could think of that would supply this kind of paraphernalia.

Now I had the perfect excuse to investigate the Curiosity Shop.

My detective work would have to be placed on hold, however, because I heard my parents calling my name from the other side of the walls. "*Gunnar! Where are you, son?*"

Oh, shoot. I needed to find a way out of there, and fast. I stealthily scrambled (as stealthily as one *can* scramble) down the right-hand pathway, past the ladder I had come down on, to a segment of wall that was held up on a swinging hinge. An exit!

I located a lever which released a lock holding it shut and pushed it open to discover that it was the backside of an empty bookshelf, and I stepped into a library on the first floor. The sound of footsteps was approaching, so I swiftly closed the secret entrance behind me, blew out my candle, and set it down on the shelf.

"There ya are, Gunnar," Pa said as he and Ma came into the room. "I coulda swore you were upstairs. Not surprised that ya found the library. S'pose you'll have these shelves filled up with books in no time."

"That's right!" I panted, out of breath from rushing. "I can buy all sorts of books now!"

"Well, don't get too worked up, boy," he replied, mistaking my heavy breathing for excitement. "We don't exactly know how lib'ral we can be with our funds yet, so any luxuries you want are gonna hafta come from your own money."

"Yeah, that sounds fair, Pa."

"Good. Worry about that later, though. What do you think of the house?"

"I love it! This house is incredible!"

"That's fine, son. Keep your shoes on, though."

"I ain't that excited, Pa."

"No, I meant that literally. There're critters in the cellar and I need your help catchin' 'em."

"...Oh..."

I decided to keep my discovery of the secret passage and the scrying room a secret. Why shouldn't I? They were an extension of my bedroom, and therefore also *my* property. Besides, I knew Pa would just get rid of the crystal ball and accompanying accessories if he found out about them. Additionally, having a secret passage to my bedroom would surely be useful.

Clearly there was a lot more for me to investigate in this town.

Chapter 8

AFTER THE EDUCATIONAL EXPERIENCE gained from disposing of rat and moth carcasses in the cellar, the subject of continuing our formal education was brought up. Rosie was too young to begin school just yet, but Ma insisted that Ellie resume her schooling. As for me, Ma and Pa both left it to my discretion. After all, I could read, write, and do arithmetic (all with exemplary skill, thank you very much).

What was left for a young man to learn?

For my purposes, everything. My curious mind was hungry to solve all the mysteries of the world around me, mysteries I was collecting like baseball cards. What better place to indulge this instinct than at school? I decided that—absolutely—I was going to continue schooling, the following morning, as a matter of fact.

The next day, I dressed myself sharply in a new pair of trousers, a white button-down shirt, and a smart vest. I combed my hair (and not with my fingers like I normally do) so I'd look very neat and handsome.

I left with my slate, chalk, and lunch in a pail, all things that Ma had bought in town the previous evening while Pa and I were trapping rats. Ellie, wearing a new dress and a bow in her hair, accompanied me and was in similarly high spirits.

Raspberry Hill Schoolhouse sat at the foot of the town's slope, on a small hill of its own. Therefore, indeed, going both to and from school, I would have to travel uphill. This was never an issue for my young legs and new shoes, but I made a mental note to use this mundane fact as a point of pride against future generations.

Although the schoolhouse did not share a building with the church—as it was in Shroud's Creek—it was remarkably similar to my old school. It's as though this sort of schoolhouse, with a bell steeple, high porch, and single room with rows of desks is the prototypical, natural form for this species of building.

My sister and I marched to the schoolhouse, hoping to present an aura of scholarliness so as to impress everyone from the start, especially the teacher.

This endeavor was apparently cursed to fail.

I could have come to that schoolhouse driven in a coach of solid gold, begemmed with rubies and sapphires, pulled by a team of white mares, and Ms. Pearson would have still assumed I was an uneducated, illiterate farm boy.

Ms. Pearson was a bitter, rigid woman with a bent spine and a crooked demeanor. She had no smooth edges, only sharp angles. Her eyes glared at you through tiny, circle-rimmed glasses that rested on her beaky nose; eyes that could out-stare a gargoyle. She was topped by flat, grey, stringy hair that was tied back so tightly it must have bitten into her flesh.

She was the sort of person who was fundamentally incurious and proud of it. Her assumption was that since she had reached a very old age, that she must have learned everything there was to know. Therefore, that it was her responsibility to make sure her students knew only what was necessary and nothing frivolous.

It mattered not if a student didn't fit into the mold, they would all be pressed into it, regardless of how it might disfigure them. To her, none of us were young minds to be instructed to think creatively and critically. Critical thought is the last thing an authoritarian teacher wants her students to learn. We were merely nails that needed a good hammering.

She and I immediately got along like oil and matches. I was stood up to be hammered before the class on that first day by way of that most dreadful and insidious of traditions: the class introduction.

"We have two new students joining us, class. This is Gunnar Shuck, and his younger sister Ellie. Tell us about yourself, young man," she ordered, spitting out the terms "new student," "young man," and "Gunnar Shuck" as if they were drops of poison on her tongue.

"Hello," I began. "I'm Gunnar, and I come from Shroud's Creek, Tennessee. I'm fourteen years old and used to work on a farm before my family lost it. We were able to come here by the generosity of my late Great-Aunt Shannon. I'm lookin' forward to gettin' to know y'all."

"LookING forward," Ms. Pearson hissed, "to meeting EVERYONE. 'Y'all' is not a word, young man."

There were obligatory giggles and chuckles from the rest of the class, a defense mechanism which all students of venomous teachers develop. Ellie performed a disappearing act by slinking into my shadow and keeping her lips buttoned.

Taken aback and impulsively defensive, I replied, "Well, you understood what I meant by it, so don't that make it a word?"

This was a grave error, for I could see demonic fire behind her eyes as she snapped, "Your grammar is atrocious, Mr. Shuck. I believe we'll have to start you on the first-grade primer and try to catch you up with the rest of the class."

"I finished up to the sixth year at my old school."

"Silence!" she sneered through lips that were not pursed so much as vaulted. "Take your seat this instant."

My combat with the teacher had spared Ellie from her wrath, and she was able to slide into an open seat undetected and unscathed.

I strolled over to an empty seat next to another boy who appeared roughly my age. He was tall and thin and had blue eyes and messy brown hair. As I sat beside him, our eyes met, and I detected sympathetic camaraderie in his. He snuck a sideways smile at me, trying simultaneously to cheer me up and conceal this display of allyship against Ms. Pearson.

Gazing about at my fellow students, I realized that my sister and I were the only red-haired ones in the room. As if we needed to be othered in more ways. Bafflingly, I caught a few of the girls stealing intrigued glances at me. I didn't consider myself a particularly attractive boy, being relatively short for my age and paler than most, but I must have still held the allure of the new kid in town.

Apparently, I had allowed my eyes to wander for too long because Ms. Pearson suddenly barked at me, "Mr. Shuck! Would you kindly answer the math problem on the board?"

The board read *422.17 - 173.09 =*. An easy one. Since the only thing this type of teacher despises more than a dumb student is a smart one, I decided to antagonize her that way.

With no hesitation, I answered, "173.09 taken from 422.17 is 249.08."

"No! Come up to the board and demonstrate how you arrived at that answer. You must have been cheating to come up with an answer that quickly."

"How could I have cheated? You just wrote it on the board."

"Unless you wish to wear the dunce cap, I recommend you come to the front of the class and explain why 422.17 - 173.09 = 249.08."

"That's what it is because it can't be nothin' else. I reckon there's only one answer to a math problem, and I got the right one. It ain't like writin' where you can answer all sortsa ways. Why should I have to wear a... 'dunce cap', you called it?"

My fellow pupils were awestruck and horrified by my words of defiance. Half of them gasped in terror, and the other half inwardly shook their heads at the foolish new boy who had no idea what kind of hornet's nest he had stepped into.

"Enough," Ms. Pearson snarled. "Outbursts like that are not to be tolerated in my classroom, especially with such careless use of contractions." She aimed her spiky finger at a stool in the corner of the room, upon which rested a paper cone with the word 'dunce' marked on it with blue ink. "You're going to sit in that chair and wear the cap until I give you permission to return to your seat. Herberth!" This caused the boy sitting next to me to shoot up like a deer who just heard a twig snap.

"Yes, ma'am!" he answered.

"Come to the front and demonstrate for your pupil how this subtraction is done."

"Yes, ma'am."

We both complied, him obediently and me begrudgingly. The rest of the class snickered at my humiliation, but the boy named Herb would occasionally flash me a glance of pity, so I knew I had at least one friend in the room. After an agonizing morning overloaded with such mistreatment, I would at long last have the chance to make friendly conversation.

Chapter 9

My hazing at the hands of Ms. Pearson carried on for the rest of the morning, until the distant ring of the church bell finally sounded, signaling the arrival of lunchtime. Now I had the opportunity to speak with my new comrade in earnest as we sat under an old apple tree in the schoolyard.

"I'm impressed Gunnar," he said while extracting a sandwich from his lunch pail, "I've never seen anyone hold their own against Ms. Pearson and live to tell about it. My name's Herberth Fort, but please, call me Herbie. Your family just moved into the big Hollinger house, right?" he asked.

With a mouthful of leftover roast beef I answered, "Yep, my great-aunt left it to us—" *gulp!* "—when she passed on."

"Mrs. Hollinger was your great-aunt, huh? Wow. You're sure lucky, Gunnar. The only thing my great-aunt left us was her old dog, and all he left was messes on the floor."

"I didn't even know I had a great-aunt until recently. Pa never mentioned her. Can you tell me what she was like?"

"Sure, everyone around here loved her, not only because she was so rich, but because she had so much… what's the word my mom used to describe when rich people have good manners? Oh yeah, 'class.' She was kind and generous to everyone, even the common folks. I wish my family was as rich as yours. My dad works at the steel mill, and mom manages the household."

"Have any brothers 'r sisters?"

"Nah, I'm the only kid at the Fort fort. When I was little, I asked them for a little brother, and they told me if I could afford one, then they'd consider it."

"Sounds like y'all are Raspberry Hill's version o' my family. We were the poorest folks in Shroud's Creek."

"Really? The way you dress and the way you spoke to Ms. Pearson, I assumed you came from a powerful Tennessee plantation family, or something."

"What's the big deal with that teacher, anyhow?" I asked before taking an angry chomp of Ma's cornbread.

"She's like that with everyone," he said, standing to pluck an apple from the branches. "Eventually you learn to just shut up and do what she says. Personally, I think she's jealous of that house of yours. She lived with her brother before she drove him to the grave, or so the kids say. Never been married, either. Can you *believe* that?"

"I think any man would get tired of bein' sent to the corner," I joked.

He laughed and replied, "They'd never get through the wedding ceremony because she'd keep correcting the pastor's grammar."

"I'd say she's an angry ol' witch, but I think she's an entirely new type o' evil critter."

Mouth full of fresh fruit, he warned, "Keep your voice down, she might hear you."

"I'm not afraid o' Ms. Pearson."

"Not her," Herbie said ominously, looking around to make sure no one was eavesdropping. "Rumor has it that there's a witch living in the woods around here."

Now, *this* had my attention. "For real? There's a bonafide witch living near this town?"

Herbie shushed me suddenly, sending apple juice dribbling down his chin. He wiped it on his sleeve and explained, "That's what some people say. Strange things happen in this town sometimes. People go missing only to turn up days later with no memory of where they'd been. Sometimes odd creatures are seen around, or normal ones act funny. One night, I thought I saw a giant walking through the forest. I think it might've been a sasquatch!"

"I thought I was the only one who saw things like that! Ever seen a stag with antlers made o' fire?"

"Er... no, not around here anyway. But one time I swear I saw a black cat take a herring from the fish market, though."

"What's so strange about that?"

"The fact that the cat brought cash to pay for it."

The rest of my school day was the same as the beginning. Ms. Pearson continued to harangue me, and I continued to be right about things. When your teacher hates you, the worst thing you can do to them is be right. I was determined to remain the wild stallion that couldn't be broken, just as Ma taught me to be.

After school, Herbie and I walked through town back to our homes. His house happened to be on the same street as mine. He told me tidbits and facts about the people who ran each store, how nice they were, and which ones were likely to call the police on you for the felony of being teen-aged in public. When we passed the Curiosity Shop, I grabbed him by the forearm to halt him.

"What can you tell me about this store?" I asked.

Herbie gave the building an apprehensive glance and murmured, "The old Curiosity Shop, huh? I don't know much about that; I've never been inside. Gives me the creeps."

"Why's that?"

He bent his narrow frame down to draw close to me and whispered, "I told you there was a witch about. Well, I think old man Mortenson might be a warlock."

"What makes you say that?" I pressed eagerly.

"If you ever see him, you'll know what I mean. I'd say he's weird, but he makes enough money that a more appropriate term would be... Well, my mom uses the word 'eccentric'. He's also pretty reclusive. You rarely ever see him around town unless someone calls on him for a service."

"He makes house calls? What for?"

Once again, Herbie looked around warily, and urged me to move away from the Curiosity Shop, in case its suspicious purveyor might be listening. We started walking again, and Herbie told me his story in a low voice.

"For instance, one time we had some kind of creature get in our cellar. It wasn't a rat or possum or raccoon; none of them make the horrifying noises this thing made. Dad wouldn't tell me what it was, but he called on Mr. Mortenson to take care of it. The old man came with a couple weird devices and a big crate.

"I wasn't allowed down there to watch, since I was a little kid when this happened, but I could hear the noises. This creature put up a fearsome fight. I could hear stuff breaking and monstrous snarling all the way from my bedroom. Eventually they managed to get it into the crate, and it was still making a ruckus when he and dad carried it out to Mortenson's carriage."

"What does he do with the critters he catches?"

"Your guess is as good as mine. Maybe he sets 'em free, maybe he has 'em stuffed and mounted. All I know is they usually aren't seen again."

"You ever see anyone buyin' things from the store?"

"Oh, sure. He sells crystals that are supposed to be good for you; powered by moonlight or magic or some such. I've also seen some houses with charms in the window that can only have come from there. Apparently, they ward off evil spirits."

"Do they work?"

"We never really see evil spirits around here—except for Ms. Pearson, that is—so I guess they must do."

We had reached the point where our paths split. Herbie lived on the east side of main street, while my house was on the west. He invited me to sit next to him in class again tomorrow. I agreed to, and he declared us to be "brothers-in-arms," now. We said farewell and parted ways.

 Chapter 10

When I returned home from school, I found my sisters playing together at the foot of the grand staircase.

"What took ya so long, Gunnar?" Ellie teased. "Didja get held after for bein' such a lousy student?"

"If my grades back at our old school weren't better'n yours, I might take offense to that," I retorted. "Plus, our old teacher wasn't nasty like this one."

"Yeah, Ms. Appleby never had a problem with us, or anyone at all. I wish there was some way we could have brought her with us from Shroud's Creek."

"Never mind Ms. Pearson, I can handle an ol' ornery teacher." I looked down and realized that my sisters were playing with new paper dolls. "Where'd you get those?"

"Ma bought these for us this morning while we were at school!" Both girls held their fashionably dressed dolls in the air for me to see. "Way better'n the corn husk dolls we used to have to play with, 'cause we didn't have to make these. She also got a new book for you, Gunnar. Somethin' called 'War of the Worlds'. Sounds violent. You'll probably love it."

"How did she convince Pa to spend the money on all that?"

"She called it a compromise. Said she wanted to get nice new stuff for us, but he didn't want to spend any extra money. But then he saw this big ol' turkey at the butcher's, and his stomach got the better of 'im. That was all she needed to get her way, in the end."

My sisters resumed their play, and I entered the kitchen to indeed discover Ma putting the finishing touches on supper. There was sweet corn and sides to accompany an enormous, steaming turkey. She was taste testing the mashed potatoes when I came in, and nearly spat them out when I suddenly appeared.

"Mmmm—" *gulp!* "—Oh, 'ey 'Ummer!" She greeted me.

Pa was nearby, rummaging in the pantry, focused intensely on a partially eaten wheel of cheddar. Some damp towels were laid out on the floor.

"Howdy, son!" He greeted me. "You seen the size o' that bird we're havin' fer supper? Ain't it somethin'? It was all my idea, y'know. Yer Ma tried to argue with me about it, but I thought we deserved to celebrate tonight, seein' as how we've made it through so much."

Ma mumbled contradiction through a mouthful of mashed potato.

"Ya don't say. Whatcha doin' in there?" I asked.

"Have you been eatin' the cheese, son?"

"No, I was at school all day."

"Right. How was school, by the way?"

"I was punished repeatedly for gettin' the right answers and usin' the words 'y'all' and 'ain't'. Also, I made a friend, or at least an ally against a common foe."

Pa was only half-listening, focused as he was on the case of the missing cheese. "That's fine, son," he muttered. "Best years of your life, schoolin', or in my case, as it often was in those days, the best *year*."

"Why d'ya ask about the cheese?" I asked.

"Cheese ain't cheap, and a big piece here has gone missin'. I asked yer Ma and sisters, but none o' 'em touched it. If it weren't you, that means we still have some critters to take care of. There's also this… liquid on the floor that I'm prayin' is just water, but thank goodness, none of it got on the cheese. I bought some mousetraps today. After supper you and I're gonna lay 'em out."

The prospect of an incontinent pest spoiled Pa's mood for the entirety of supper. Ma's roast turkey was the most delicious thing I had ever eaten, yet Pa couldn't keep his mind off the cheese wheel in the pantry. He glared into the kitchen, waiting like a cat for the slightest disturbance to pounce on.

Of course, nothing was heard or seen all through the meal. Afterward, I helped him cover the floor and several shelves with mousetraps. Many were also placed at strategic locations around the house on all floors. Incidentally, this required us to use more cheese as bait than was actually stolen. His argument was that would be made up for in future cheese whose theft would be prevented.

Several days passed, and the dairy-based robbery continued without any sign of the culprit. Each afternoon, Pa and I would reconvene at home to find that some traps had indeed been sprung, but the bait was missing, and the only thing left behind was a small puddle of salty water and some soggy crumbs of cheddar.

Late at night, I could faintly hear what sounded like sobbing and whimpering coming from the other side of the walls. As upset as Pa had been made by the ordeal, I knew it wasn't him crying. He wasn't the sort of man who possessed the ability. I had the presence of mind to look into my secret passageway, but by the time I could light a candle to check, the sound and its source had vanished.

Several traps were sprung accidentally by my father, whose anger and desperation were steadily increasing alongside the number of bruises on his feet. Finally at wits end, Pa considered hiring a ratcatcher. To his dismay, no one offered that service in Raspberry Hill, and sending away to Harrisburg for one would cost more than Pa cared to spend.

It was here that I cunningly seized the opportunity that I had been waiting for.

"Y'know, Pa," I said to him at breakfast, "there is *one* business in town that offers an exterminatin' service, o' sorts."

"Which one is that?" growled Pa, while applying ointment to his stinging toes.

"Mr. Levi Mortenson down on Main Street. He advertises in his windows that he catches critters."

"Mortenson…? Ain't that the weird old man that sells voodoo and that sorta nonsense?"

"He ain't weird, Pa. He's *eccentric*."

"…Ya mean he talks funny?"

"No, 'eccentric' is what you call a feller who acts strange but has money."

"That what they're learnin' ya at school? Well, you can call me weird, 'cuz I don't care what words you use for it; I don't want that geezer in our house."

"My friend Herb said he once helped his Pa catch, oh… I think it was a bobcat when it got into their cellar."

"There's bobcats around here?"

"There was in the Fort house, and Mr. Mortenson was able to catch it. Should be a breeze to capture some cheese-snatching rats. Besides, it'll be way cheaper than sendin' out to Harrisburg."

"Fine," Pa relented. "I'll go by there today and talk to 'im. After that, I don't never want to hear about that old man again. Can't be dealin' with folks that're weird *and* eccentric."

True to his word, Pa returned that afternoon and informed us that he had described the strange circumstances we had encountered to Mr. Mortenson. Apparently, the old man immediately knew what we had here and agreed to come capture the thing. He would be arriving at the house the following morning.

It was a Saturday, and I was alone in the house. I had no school, but Pa worked, and Ma had gone to the market and taken my sisters along. Pa had asked me to keep an eye on things and wait for Mortenson to arrive, and to shut down any funny business.

I was seated comfortably in the library, enjoying my book about critters from Mars attacking Earth, when a knock came at the door. Eagerly I dashed to the entrance, prepared myself mentally, took a deep breath, and threw the doors open.

Chapter 11

I OPENED THE DOOR to find myself face-to-face with a beard.

Except it wasn't just a beard; there was an entire man attached to it, but it had a life and presence all its own which hit you like a cannonball. That beard and the moustache intertwined with it were altogether a snowy-white waterfall of facial hair that cascaded all the way to the floor, and further still.

If a detective were trying to discern the difference between my footprints and his, they'd have no need to look at the pattern left by our shoes, but by the trail his beard would make as it brushed along behind him.

Above these overflowing whiskers, greyish-blue eyes gazed out at me through circle-rimmed glasses. They sat beneath the shadow of a bowler hat atop his wispy white hair, past wrinkles and crow's feet that contoured his face. These eyes—brimming with the wisdom of years and a lifetime of mischief—froze me to the spot like a gorgon's stare.

The man attached to the beard was tall, but the effect of his height was ruined by the crook in his neck which caused him to hunch forward. He supported his lopsided body on a well-used wooden cane and was dressed sharply in a black suit with grey pinstripes. This was a man who was not merely old; he was an ancient relic. Methuselah's grandfather.

The fingers on his other hand tapped impatiently on

the handles of a pair of nested buckets which contained a stack of towels. I realized then that I had been standing there for some time, taking in the multifaceted strangeness of this visitor. To my embarrassment, he noticed before I did.

"Well, boy?" he demanded in a gravelly, yet surprisingly ferocious voice. "Are you going to invite me in or keep staring at me like I'm a garish and tasteless porch ornament?"

I snapped out of my stupor then and held the door open as he entered my home. Before I had the chance to say a word, he thrust his bowler hat into my hands, which I accepted and hung on the hat rack in the foyer. He took a brief look around, then turned to me and spoke again.

"You must be the son of that fellow that asked me to come yesterday."

"Er, yeah, my name is Gunnar Shuck," I answered nervously.

"Is it really? I suppose there's nothing to be done about that now. You may call me Mr. Mortenson. Is Mr. Shuck in today?"

"Pa's at work. I'm mannin' the house today."

"That's perfectly suitable. It makes no difference who it is as long as there's at least one able-bodied person about to assist me. Your father said you had a mysterious beast lurking?"

"Um, that's right. For the past several days, bits of our cheese have gone missin', and we keep findin' these... *puddles* around. Oh, also I can sometimes hear a noise like somethin's cryin' on the other side of the wall."

"That's what your father described to me yesterday, except he didn't mention any crying. That confirms my initial hunch." He shoved the buckets into my hands, started hobbling up the stairs with unexpected swiftness, and beckoned me to follow him with a wave of his hand. His beard flapped as it dragged up each step.

"Off we go, then. Shouldn't give us too much trouble so long as you follow the instructions I give you."

"Wait... So, you reckon you know what it is, then?" I asked while scrambling to keep up with the surprisingly quick old man.

"Indeed, I do."

"...Can you tell me what it is?"

He scoffed and replied, "You couldn't possibly be prepared to believe it."

"You'd be surprised at the things I'm prepared to believe."

"I'm never surprised."

"Not by anything, huh? I know I was surprised, fr' instance, when I saw a deer with antlers made o' fire back in Tennessee."

That stopped him mid-step. Ominously, he turned to me and asked, "You've seen a Not-Deer?"

"That's what someone had called it in a book I found. You know about it, then?"

"It's an exceedingly rare creature, hardly ever seen by man."

"I caught it settin' fire to our crops one night when I was younger. It's the reason we had to leave and come here."

Mr. Mortenson gave this some thought, then continued climbing and answered, "That *is* surprising. In light of this, I think you may be seaworthy, so to speak. Enough at least for me to tell you what we're dealing with here."

"Great! What is it?"

He sighed, leaned in close to me, and answered, "It's a squonk."

"...Gesundheit?"

"I didn't sneeze! The creature you have here is called a squonk."

"Squonk, huh? That's an odd name for a critter."

"And Gunnar Shuck is an odd name for a boy. A name is a name, even if it sounds silly to you."

"And that's a real critter, y'say? You're not just pullin' my leg?"

"Trust me, all of your limbs remain undisturbed."

"What's a squonk look like, then?" I challenged him as we reached the second floor and continued down the hall.

"A squonk is raccoon-sized, piggish, and hideously ugly. It cries nearly all the time because it's self-conscious and ashamed of its ghastly appearance. That's the reason for the missing cheese and the sobbing. It's eating to distract itself from its feelings of self-pity."

"I've looked high and low, and I've never seen anythin' like that."

"You wouldn't. The squonk is a very shy creature, extremely cautious and elusive."

"We've been trying to catch it with mousetraps."

"Hoho!" He chuckled with a Clausian twinkle in his eye. "How amusing. Trying to catch a squonk by conventional means is utterly futile. If caught, it will dissolve into a pool of tears to escape."

"That explains what the buckets and towels are for, then."

"Did you think I was here to wash your windows?"

"I didn't think—" I started but was shushed by the old man.

He reached into his suit coat pocket and produced a thin brass horn. He pressed the bell-end of this apparatus to the wall and inserted the other end into his ear. I watched him scrunch up his eyes and mouth to help him focus, but after several seconds of listening, he relaxed his features and muttered, "Not there..."

He crept along the wall at several positions, gradually approaching the door to my bedroom. I became worried that I would have to reveal my hidden passageway and give up my favorite secret. Finally, he came to a point on the wall and his eyes lit up.

"Eureka!" he whispered. "Here, lad. Take a listen to this."

I leaned sideways into the ear-horn and listened. Sure enough, there was a strange noise on the other side.

Sob-sob, crunch chew-chew, sob-sob...

"Sounds like cryin' and eatin'," I responded softly.

Cryptid Currency

"That's a squonk if ever I heard one," Mortenson said.

"Dealt with a lot of these, then?"

"It's one of the more common cryptids in this region. You won't have even heard of them in Okabedokee, Tennessee, or wherever it is you said you came from."

"Shroud's Creek, thank you very much. Okabedokee is downriver."

"Either way, it makes me the expert on squonks, by proxy."

"Fair enough. So, how do we catch it?"

"Do you have a washroom with a bathtub?"

"Yes, it's down the hall on the left."

"Excellent. Run, boy, and fetch some cheese, a stick of butter, and meet me there."

He took the buckets from me and ran off before I could protest. I went to the pantry to do as he asked, although I was somewhat confused. The cheese made sense, that was obviously bait. But the butter? Were we trapping the squonk, or preparing to bake it?

I just had to hope that Mr. Mortenson really knew what he was doing, and the end of our dairy dilemma was drawing to a close.

I cut a wedge of cheddar and placed it on a dish. Next, I grabbed a butter knife, opened the ice box, and scooped out a few sizable heaps of butter onto the plate. Returning to the washroom, I found Mortenson stuffing the rubber stopper into the drain in our claw-foot tub. He had placed one of the buckets upside-down on the floor and the pile of hand towels nearby.

"Excellent, lad," he said, taking the dish from me and holding the cheese up to examine. "A finely aged cheddar you have there. That will be sure to draw out the squonk." He placed it gingerly in the center of the tub.

"What's the butter for?" I asked.

"Spread it around the rim of the tub. That way it won't be able to climb out once its inside."

"So, we're going to lure it into the tub and trap it there?"

"Precisely! Get it nice and slippery while I lay out a trail of cheese crumbs."

I started using the butter knife to coat the tub, but when the old man saw me doing this, he laughed and said there was no reason to be so delicate. *'Get your hands dirty, so to speak,'* is what he said. Once the tub (and my hands) were thoroughly coated with butter, Mortenson gave me one final instruction.

"Now, lad, I see you have a closet here. There's only room within for one, and it looks like you'll fit comfortably inside, being so short."

"Oh, *bless yer heart*; yer so kind; thank ya," I replied with all the southern sarcasm I could muster.

"That's very good of you to say," he obliviously replied. "I'll wait around the corner. Once you hear the squonk get into the tub, holler for me. Get ready, now!"

He left me alone to crouch in the closet by myself. Contrary to his assumption, I was still cramped in there, like a sandwich made of towels, a broom, and dustpan. While I was wiping my buttery hands on a towel and feeling increasingly silly, I heard an approaching noise.

Sniff-sniff... chomp! Sniff-sniff... chomp! **Sniff-sniff... chomp!**

I couldn't tell if it was smelling the bait or whimpering to itself, but regardless, it was surely the squonk heading into our trap. I heard the pitter-patter of tiny paws on the tin bucket, then a slippery squeaking as it leapt into the tub and slid down the edge. It padded around for a minute, then stopped moving and started munching on the cheese between whiny gasps of air.

This was it. Not since my encounter with the not-deer had I felt so invigorated. I delicately raised my hand to the closet door and drew in a deep breath to ready myself, and pounced.

Chapter 12

Not since Napolean's defeat at Waterloo had an attack been so poorly executed. In my haste to exit the closet, my arm caught the broom, which yanked the entire stack of towels down from the shelf overhead, and everything came crashing down. A towel draped over my head as I and the entire business came tumbling out onto the washroom floor.

"Mr. Mortenson, help! It's in the tub," I called out, panicking as I wrestled with the towel.

The ruckus spooked the squonk, and I heard it frantically scramble to try and climb out of the tub. The sound of porcelain squeaking let me know that our trap was working. Its paws slipped on the butter on every side, but could find no purchase, sending it sliding back down.

The squonk was caught!

The old man rejoined me in the washroom, bursting with enthusiasm. "Well done, lad. You've caught the little beastie. Quit playing with that towel now and have a look for yourself."

I threw the towel on the floor, peered over the rim of the tub, and got my first glimpse of the creature that had been harassing my family all week.

The squonk was not large. True to what Mortenson had said earlier, it was roughly the size of a raccoon. It had the rotund body and face of a pig, and the limbs and tail of a monkey. Its entire body was covered with patchy, scratchy, putrid-brown hair and its skin with all manner of warts, boils, and unnamable blemishes that came in an assortment of sizes and colors.

While I was regarding it with conspicuous revulsion, it stared back at me with pitiful, tear-filled eyes, and curled into a pathetic little ball. I tried to unscrew my face at it, but its lower lip began to quiver, compounding my remorse. The squonk buried its unfortunate face in its fuzzy hands and wept noisily and moistly.

Honestly, I felt quite guilty for having apparently hurt its feelings so badly.

Mr. Mortenson noticed the look of pity on my face, and said, "Don't feel bad, son. Just watch what it'll do."

It was then that the squonk began to transform. All of the color on its body drained away and became translucent. Its form melted into undefined blobs of fluid as it transitioned from solid to liquid. With a final sob and a sniffle, it sloshed into a puddle and settled in the tub.

The pool of liquid circled the tub, seeking an escape route. Unfortunately for it, however, the drain was blocked, and it had no way out. The squonk-puddle bubbled in frustration.

"See?" Mortenson said as he waved his cane accusingly at the watery animal. "It was just trying to escape. Mercy is a fine quality to have, lad, but there are those who will try to take advantage of you for it. Grab the towels, now, and help me get it into the buckets."

We worked for a while, soaking up every drop of the squonk and wringing it out into both buckets. Mr. Mortenson assured me that it wouldn't be able to get away now, since it couldn't reassume its solid form until it was alone, and no one was looking at it. In a day of bizarre experiences, handling the warm, salty, cognizant fluid was by far the weirdest.

How did I know it was salty? Embarrassingly, during the process of soaking it up and squeezing it into my bucket, I had forgotten that it was once a creature of flesh and blood, and absent-mindedly wiped my face while it covered my hands. I had to spit to get the saline taste out of my mouth when I realized my mistake, which Mortenson found delightfully amusing.

At points I swear it was looking at me, and with contempt, no less.

Once we had two buckets full of liquid squonk, Mortenson had me carry them down the stairs to the front entrance of the manor. He retrieved his hat from the stand and replaced it on his head.

"Thanks for the help today, son. Be sure to keep the true nature of what we dealt with today a secret, hm? People have a hard time believing in the fantastical and I don't want to hear you wound up in an asylum later on."

"Trust me, I already learned that lesson the hard way," I replied.

"Ah, very well. When it comes to the scrutiny of skeptics, I believe it's best to be inoculated at a young age, anyway."

"What're you going to do with the critter?" I asked.

"A squonk is a harmless, but nonetheless bothersome beast, so I'll keep it safe in my shop for a time until I can locate its nest and return it."

"If it comes back, can I catch it the same way again?"

"Most surely. A squonk isn't the brightest of creatures and can be fooled the same way multiple times."

The bucket boiled with self-righteous anger.

"Quiet, you. Now, I really must be going. I'll send an invoice to your father later on."

Mortenson leaned over and tried to lift a bucket in each hand while clutching his cane under his arm. He grunted and groaned from the weight but could barely raise them off the floor. He shifted to holding the cane in one hand and the handles of both buckets in the other, but this was an even more futile endeavor. Amazingly, not a drop of squonk dripped to the floor.

It was here that I seized an opportunity.

"Looks like you're strugglin' with those," I hinted.

"Balderdash," He barked. "I'm not as spry as I once was, but I can still carry a paltry... *grrrrrr*... little...

hrnnnnnnn... bucketful of squonk or two!" *Pant, wheeze...*

"Mr. Mortenson, why don'tcha let me help you carry those back to your shop? I don't have anythin' else to do today. I'd be glad to be useful."

After one more spine-crunching attempt, the old man relented. "Very well," he said. "I will accept your help, this once. But try to keep up! I can't have you falling behind and embarrassing yourself."

Finally, the moment I had been waiting for was nearly here. I had a plausible excuse to enter the place Pa had expressly forbidden.

At long last, I was going to see the inside of the Curiosity Shop.

# Chapter 13

Mortenson paraded on down the road ahead of me, laughing and gloating all the way. "Move along smartly, lad, but be careful not to spill those buckets."

The squonk buckets were heavier than I had expected them to be. I'd carried plenty of heavy loads on the old farm, but this was an animal in fluid form, not just ordinary water. It deliberately sloshed back and forth to throw me off balance. That was all it could do to spite me, limited as its capacity for retaliation was.

Determined to show that I was capable to the boasting old man—who was gleefully unaware of how I struggled—I resolved not to make a peep despite it all. Still, I occasionally had to pause to rest my arms, for which the squonk bubbled mockingly at me.

Pride forbade me from relenting, however. It was a pride all men inherit from their cave-dwelling ancestors, who would compete to see who could carry the largest boulder without grunting a single complaint. While technological advancements have rendered this practice unnecessary, culture has staggered to keep up and the custom continues to this day.

My biggest concern, though, was how this might look to a casual observer. I was prepared to make up some sort of story to explain this situation if anyone stopped us, whether they be onlooker or policeman. What reason *could* one give to explain why a reclusive Curiosity Store owner and fourteen-year-old boy were carrying buckets full of mystery fluid down the street? To my surprise, however, no one bothered us.

Sure, every townsperson we passed gave sidelong, suspicious looks to the galivanting eccentric and his red-headed follow-along with the buckets of who-knows-what. Perhaps it was Mortenson's reputation that made them think twice about asking questions. He surpassed a certain threshold of strangeness that simply went beyond most people's capacity for inquiry.

Finally, we arrived at the Curiosity Shop without stoppage or spillage, and the old man unlocked the door.

In my wild imagination, I dreamed that the interior would be a circus of supernatural wonders: shelves stretching all the way to the ceiling, packed with strange relics that glowed and hummed with magical potential. Perhaps they would even float through the air! I pictured a series of cages on one wall, hosting a menagerie of strange creatures.

It is doubtful that the shop could have lived up to these otherworldly expectations, but I hadn't prepared myself for the possibility that the shop interior would be so... ordinary.

Sure, the wares were unusual, and I wouldn't have been able to name most of the objects on sale, but the shop itself was no different from any other, curious or otherwise. As was to be expected, neat rows of shoulder-high shelves lined the shop floor, stocked with products. There was an aroma of fruits and spices blended with rotting driftwood and old leather.

The window at the front seemed to hold the most interesting items, like beaded and feathered baubles, glimmering trinkets, and vials with skulls and crossbones on them. Those were all tucked behind the checkout counter, where a curious customer would have no choice but to ask about them, and then be ambushed by a sales pitch. A black cat was guarding (or at least sleeping next to) the cash register.

"Glad to see you're keeping a watchful eye over things,

Ysabel," Mortenson teased her.

In response, she cracked open one yellow eye, reproachfully glared at him, then yawned and rolled over to resume her slumber.

"I wouldn't have expected any less from you."

I was led to the back of the store, where a staircase—which led to the apartment above—hung over a single cast-iron door. He removed a rusted iron key from his coat pocket and unlocked it. Before I could follow him in, he spun around and blocked my entry through and view of what lay beyond it.

"Thank you very much for your assistance, lad. I'll take those from here," he said, extending his hands.

I tried to peek around him but could not quite make out what was in the room beyond. There was a light coming from within, but something about it was... off somehow. I could faintly hear the distant sound of chains rattling and wood thumping on wood.

I asked, "Is somethin' back there?"

"Don't worry about that noise," he insisted. "That's just the, er... building settling. Old foundation and what-have-you."

"You sure you don't need any more help? I can carry the buckets in there for you," I offered, not at all convinced by his weak explanation, and now more curious than ever.

"No, no, I can handle this. Don't worry about me."

That was the only bargaining chip I could think of to get me inside, and it failed. Reluctantly, I handed the buckets over to him, and he swung quickly around to set them down on the other side of the door.

"Don't leave just yet though. I have something for you." He swept his trailing beard behind him so it wouldn't get caught in the door when he slammed it shut. The last thing I heard was the muffled clanking of the lock re-engaging and several bolts clicking into place.

Oh, well. If I couldn't see inside the mysterious door, I might as well have a look around the shop and peruse its wares.

Chapter 14

Earlier I wrote that the Curiosity Shop was ordinary. This was true only as it pertains to the layout. The items for sale were anything but. While waiting for Mr. Mortenson to return from the storeroom, I strolled the aisles, examining the bizarre sundries they displayed.

On a shelf labelled "Remedies" were a plethora of strange medicines. One bottle advertised itself as "*Sandman Sleeping Pills, a cure for insomnia, headaches, noisy children, and sometimes all three at once*". Another claimed to be a potion for exorcising malicious spirits, demonic possessions, and toothaches.

There were tiny drawstring bags with "Anti-Hex Charm" embroidered on them. Peering inside one of them, I discovered a bundle of twigs, grasses, dried fruits, and spices. Well, if it didn't ward off evil spells, at least it would provide the room with a pleasant aroma.

Further along, there was a shelf loaded with rocks and crystals of every description. A glittering purple jewel was purported to be a cure for illnesses of the stomach, although it came with a disclaimer that it was most effective when used with doctor-prescribed medicine. One milky-white gem had a tag that simply said "Moon Crystal," but did not elaborate. There was a solid block of salt that instructed the buyer to *"grind and spread across windows and doorways to block the entry of evil spirits, or sprinkle on food for seasoning."*

The foremost shelf at the entrance to the store was

stocked with an assortment of aromatic candles. Either they were the most popular item on sale, or they were placed there to cover up the scent of ancient architecture. They came in a variety of colors and scents, from peppermint and strawberry to black licorice and cinnamon, and something called "Romantic Picnic by the Seaside," which had grains of sand in the tallow but merely smelled of cheap soap.

Next, I approached the cashier's counter where Ysabel the black cat was still snoozing. There was a jar of unusual sweets labelled *"Complementary Fortune Cookies – The latest thing from distant ~~Japan~~ China! Find out what the future holds in store for you!"* I helped myself to one of these, cracking it open and discovering a tiny slip of paper within. I read the premonition on it:

BEWARE, YOU WILL SOON MEET A FRIGHTENING STRANGER.

I was horrorstruck until I flipped it over and read:

Product of Smith's Confectionaries, San Francisco, CA

My fears alleviated, I crunched on the dry, mildly sweet cookie, and turned my attention to Ysabel. She was smaller than the squonk was, with shiny, midnight-black fur. Her body was curled into a donut, and she squeaked as she snored. I was compulsively tempted to pet her.

"Hi, kitty-kitty," I cooed. She flicked one ear and remained asleep.

"Kitty-kitty, who's a good kitty?" I repeated. This time, she turned her head and pointed the yellow slits of her eyes at me, regarding me with annoyance. I held out my hand for her to smell, and she stared offended at it like I had presented her with a dead rat.

"Are you a good girl, Ysabel?" I asked.

"...Meow..." Ysabel said disdainfully.

As I reached out my hand to pat her on the head, I was

suddenly interrupted by the re-appearance of Mr. Mortenson.

"I wouldn't do that if I were you," He warned. "Ysabel doesn't trust strangers and isn't afraid to scratch or bite."

The cat licked her paw as if to scoff at me.

With the old man back, I could resume my ploy to pry into his secrets. I thought flattery might gain me some advantage, so I said, "I was just lookin' around. This is a mighty fine store you have here."

"Yes, I know it is. Here, this for you." He held out a slip of paper with a list of services rendered and a total charge at the bottom. "It's an invoice. See to it that your father receives it and pays my fee."

"Oh," I sighed.

"Also, let him know I accept cash, precious metals, and jewels."

"I'm near certain we ain't got any jewels."

"Most don't. However, I like to give people options. Not credit, though. Don't trust it. I can't buy bread with credit."

"I'll make sure Pa gets this."

"You seem disappointed somehow. Did you imagine that I was going to give you some kind of repayment for today? Nothing in life is free, hmm?"

I folded the invoice, putting it in my pocket with my complementary fortune. "No, that's fair. You don't owe me anything. Unless..." I had an idea at that moment, and risky though it was, it was too tempting not to try it. "Unless you hire me on as a shop assistant!"

"I beg your pardon?" Mortenson gasped, his beard bristling at the very notion.

"Hire me on. I can do all sorts of work. I can carry heavy things, clean, and I'm good at sums. I think you could use some help around here and I'd love to—"

"No. I don't need any help," he interrupted. "I'm perfectly fine with things as they are."

"But, today, you couldn't even lift the buckets, and there's no way you can run the whole store by yourself."

"I've run this store single-handedly for years, thank

you very much. Besides, I'm not alone. Ysabel is here to lend a paw."

"Meow," said Ysabel in agreement.

"Come on, just give me a chance," I protested.

"No, no, a thousand times no! I thank you for your assistance today," he insisted, escorting me out of the store via the under-the-arm method, "but rest assured that despite my age, I'm perfectly capable of running the Curiosity Shop without anyone's help. Now please leave, so I can tend to my business."

I conceded that I had lost this battle, but I was determined not to lose the war. I obediently returned back to the street and mundane normalcy.

As the door closed behind me, I thought I heard Mortenson say to his cat, "*Would you have decided differently? I can't just let* anyone *in. It's too dangerous to...*" and then silence as the door shut.

# Chapter 15

Well, dear reader, you should know me well enough by now to predict that I wouldn't let that be the end of it. Whatever could possibly be so dangerous that I should be kept away from it? This only intrigued me further. I needed to gather more information.

Next door to the Curiosity Shop was Tumble's Drugstore, and Mr. Tumble himself was standing in the doorway, sweeping out the dust before closing. If anyone had an embarrassment of the old man's secrets, surely it was his next-door neighbor.

Mr. Tumble was a cylindrical man, shaped like a tin can from the base to the peak, and topped by a perfectly round, shiny, bald head. He had a handlebar mustache and a distant, tired look in his eyes that suggested that he had heard of sleep but had never personally encountered it.

Clinging to his shoulder was an iguana, which dug its claws into his blue-striped shirt to maintain its perch. It twisted around and slanted its head quizzically as I approached the druggist.

"Excuse me, sir, but do you know anythin' about the Curiosity Shop next door?" I asked.

Without turning his attention away from his sweeping, he answered, "Old Man Mortenson's Curiosity Shop, eh? Can't say I've been in there, myself, but my wife is fond of his aromatic candles. Did you know that a romantic picnic by the seaside smells just like soap?"

The druggist possessed a rational mind. That is to say,

he had to ration his thoughts carefully lest he should expend his limited supply.

"*Bless yer heart*; I didn't; thank ya," I sarcastically replied. "Can you tell me anythin' else about the shop or Mr. Mortenson?"

"He's been running that shop for a long time. Since before I was born, I know that much. I remember back when I was a little lad and Poppa Tumble ran the drugstore, we used to see him go in and out of his shop, sometimes with these great, big crates. Heaven knows what was in them. That was forty-odd years ago, and he hasn't changed a bit."

Tumble's demeanor suddenly shifted. He brought his eyebrows tightly together, trying to make what he just said add up. He gave up after several awkward moments, shrugged and continued, "I guess that must mean the stuff he sells actually works. Otherwise, an old man like him wouldn't still be around and about like that. Sometimes I'll hear strange noises from the shop, like sparks of electricity or some thumping, but I suppose it's none of my business."

"Ever see any really odd critters comin' or goin'?"

"Hmmm... Not that I can think of. Let's ask Spot if he's seen anything." He turned to the lizard on his shoulder and asked, "Hey, Spot, seen anything strange over there?"

The iguana stuck out its forked tongue and licked its master on the cheek. I respectfully faked a laugh, but apparently Mr. Tumble was not joking.

"Come on, Spot, why don't you say something?" he complained.

I took a step back and said, "Er, Mr. Tumble, does your iguana talk to you?"

"Is that what you are, Spot? Well, I suppose iguanas *don't* talk, do they? Don't look at me like that. Everyone talks to their pets, and sometimes they *do* answer."

"I see... Well, thank you kindly for your time, sir. I won't be disturbed—I mean, won't disturb you any longer."

Odd man, him. Either there really was something else going on in the Curiosity Shop, or eccentricity was contagious. I made my way back up the street to return home. From our porch at the top of the hill, I searched down toward the bottom of town and found the back of the Curiosity Shop. As I gazed down at it, I swear something peculiar happened: Either the colors of the sunset were playing tricks with my eyes, or the alleyway next to the shop was flashing with staccato bolts of purple and green.

People around here must have been incredibly oblivious or else conditioned to ignore Mortenson's hijinks. I couldn't decide which was more likely.

At home, I found that the supper table was set, and my family was waiting for me. As soon as I sat down, Pa interrogated me about the day's events.

"So, Gunnar, did that Levi Mortenson come by today?"

"He did, Pa," I answered, handing him the slip of paper. "Here's his invoice."

His eyes shot out like cannonballs when he read it. "CON-found it! That's a steep fee. Tell me he actually caught the critter."

"He sure did, Pa, and I helped. I guarantee you no one else in the world would have known how to catch it."

"What in tarnation was it?"

"It was a squo—a skunk."

"A skunk? I've dealt with those before, and I didn't smell nothin' like any skunk."

"It was a, er... northern skunk. Different from the ones we had in Tennessee."

"If you say so, son," Pa said while shoveling a spoonful of beef stew into his mouth. "Just glad to have the dagnabbed thing gone."

"Say, Pa..." I started, almost hesitating to ask my next question.

"Yes?"

"What would you think about me takin' on an after-school job?"

A proud smile spread across Pa's face, and he

answered, "I reckon that's a fine idea, son. Y' could bring in some extra money for yerself, that way."

"As long as you don't neglect your schoolin'," Ma added.

"That ain't a problem. All I have to do is get the right answers, and so far, I know 'em all. I can probably learn more from workin' than I can from Ms. Pearson."

"That's m'boy!" Pa beamed, giving the table a celebratory thunk. "Can't no one keep down the plucky Shucks! Where'd you have in mind to work at, anyway?"

"Oh, there're plenty o' good stores in town that could use an assistant."

"Long as you don't go into that Curiosity Shop again. Still don't trust that Mortenson fella, an' I don't wantcha comin' home smellin' like Pennsylvania skunk every day."

I tightened my lips. Pa's approval was a fickle thing, and I was not about to admit my true intentions. If I did, Pa would make me promise not to go near there, a promise I'd have to break. Conveniently, there's no reason to feel bad about breaking a promise that you didn't make in the first place.

There would be church tomorrow morning, and no businesses—including Mortenson's—would be open on a Sunday. First thing after school on Monday though, I was going to go straight back to the Curiosity Shop and demand a job there. He couldn't say "no" forever, but I was stubborn enough to ask for that long.

Chapter 16

School was the same as always, that Monday. The only difference was that I went out of my way to be a perfect, angelic pupil so that I could avoid getting into trouble. Ms. Pearson was in the habit of holding me after class for the most trivial of slights, real or imagined. This happened with such dependable regularity that my parents were confused when I came home from school *on time*.

I was forced to write lines on the board so frequently that my right arm built considerable muscle. By the same process, I perfected a style of handwriting so quick and illegible as to put doctors to shame. The dunce cap had become as much a part of my wardrobe as my overalls and vests. I wore it like a crown.

I was the jar lid that refused to come unscrewed, no matter how much Ms. Pearson twisted me. Because of this, I immediately became her most hated student. This was a new experience for me, and not one I savored.

The other students had gotten used to this arrangement and regarded me as a sort of karmic sponge, a lightning rod that drew the teacher's ire away from them. Even my sister, Ellie, who had settled nicely into the school routine and joined a group of friends her age, pretended not to know me when class was in session.

I can't blame my fellow pupils for not coming to my defense. I wasn't Spartacus, and they weren't my troops. They were children, afraid of the wrath of a venomous old woman who wielded enormous power over them. There would be time to organize a revolution later (for decades students would speak in hushed, reverent tones about the Great Passive-Aggression of 1901.)

By holding my tongue between my gritted teeth, I was able to avoid punishment. After school, I raced out of the doors and up Main Street, carried on the wings of anticipation. But before I entered the Curiosity Shop, I noticed something odd. It was Mr. Tumble, wiping the glass windows on his storefront. His animal companion was also worthy of note.

The iguana that had been riding on his shoulder the other day had been replaced by a vibrant multicolored parrot. The bird similarly clutched him with its talons like the lizard had, and occasionally flapped its wings and nibbled at his ear.

When it saw me, it flashed me a beaky smile and squawked, *"Braaaaaawk! Bless your heart, bless your heart! Braaawk!"*

I approached the druggist and said, "Afternoon, Mr. Tumble. D'you remember me?"

Without looking at me, he answered, "Yes, of course. You're the young man who wanted to know about the Curiosity Shop. Did you have any other questions for me?"

"Only one, right now. Do you collect exotic animals?"

"Exotic…? Nope, just this parrot, here."

"But didn't you have an iguana the other day?"

"That might be the case. I have a hard time keeping it straight, but I know for sure the only animal I own is old Spot, here."

"Braaaaawk! Spotty want a cricket!" the parrot shrieked.

"Sounds like he has a hankerin' for crickets," I responded.

"Are you sure he didn't say *cracker*? That's what a parrot would normally ask for."

"No, he said he wanted a cricket, which is what iguanas eat."

"Well, Spot, you ate all the crickets when you were an iguana, and you'll just have to settle for a cracker now."

"*Braaaaaawk! Cricket, cracker! Braaaaaawk!*"

"Is Spot a different animal from day to day, Mr. Tumble?"

"Yes, the silly creature can't seem to make up his mind what he wants to be. I let him outside to do his business at night and he comes back a totally different animal." The druggist leaned against the door and wistfully twiddled his mustache. "Sometimes he's a mammal, sometimes a bird, and sometimes a reptile. This isn't the first time he was a parrot. He's been many different breeds of dog. One time, he was even an elephant!"

"Wow, I'd like to see that."

Mr. Tumble winked and replied, "Be careful what you wish for, my boy. Back in my day, to 'see the elephant' meant you'd learned something that came at a great personal cost. I really saw the elephant that day, believe me. I remember it well, and I guess Spot would too if he still *was* one."

"*Braaaaawk! Get off that shelf! Get off that shelf!*"

"Seems he does," chuckled the bird's owner. "I'm glad we can laugh about it now, Spotty, old boy."

"D'you remember what he was when you got 'im?" I asked, trying to keep this deranged conversation on the rails.

"You know, I don't believe I *can* recall that. Not that it matters anymore now, though. Whatever he was back then isn't important, it's what he is now that is. I try my darndest to be patient with him while he's going through his changes and take care of him as best I can."

"Lucky he has you to take care of 'im."

"Thank you, son. Wish I could have had that kind of choice when I was a boy. I've always wanted to see what's it's like to be another animal. Come to think of it, every now and then I have these peculiar dreams where I'm a squirrel. I go hopping around in the forest, collecting acorns, climbing trees, washing laundry... You know, the usual squirrel activities."

"That's very... int'restin', Mr. Tumble," I said, seeking a swift escape from the conversation. "I won't take any more o' your time now. Thank you. It's certainly been... educational."

"Any time, lad! Kids these days are so polite..." he drifted off into his musings as I turned to leave him to them.

I had a theory as to the cause of Spot's shape shifting. Perhaps there was magic spilling out of the shop that was affecting him. Judging by the drugstore's proximity to the Curiosity Shop, the strange lights I saw a few evenings ago, and Tumble's routine of letting his pet out at night, it seemed the natural conclusion that the changes were caused by magic.

The assumption being, of course, that magic was real. What other explanation could there be, though?

This confirmed for me that further infiltration into Mortenson's business was warranted. I now had a moral obligation to investigate the cause of Spot's transformations. What if Spot found himself one night transformed into a trout stranded on the sidewalk? Or a fly caught in a spider's web? The welfare of a supernaturally affected animal was at stake.

With my new and convenient excuse, I advanced on the Curiosity Shop.

Chapter 17

I ENTERED THE STORE to find its purveyor aggressively trying to convince a customer, the only other human occupant of the building, to make a purchase. Ysabel the black cat was perched on a shelf overhead, watching the scene unfold with passive interest and a dash of smugness.

The customer—a man with a lip-obscuring mustache who wore his Sunday best every day of the week—was trapped in conversation with Mr. Mortenson. According to the rules of social engagement, one cannot simply remove themselves from an unwanted interaction. This has to be accomplished by offering some plausible excuse as to why you can't stay, or by insisting that *you* are somehow the one inconveniencing your captor and should release them immediately.

Visibly sweating, the poor fellow was seeking some polite way to break away from the conversation so that he could make an exit with his wallet intact.

"I tell you truly, Mr. Graham, no one from here to the Atlantic coast sells better medicines and remedies than the ones I have here," the old man boasted. "Just look at the wide variety of potions, tinctures, ointments and pills I have to offer."

The customer stammered, "Er, um, what about the drugstore next door? I don't want to take up any more of your time, so I think I'll look there and—"

"Conventional medicine is all well and good; fine stuff, but what I have are time-proven remedies that go all the way back to the ancient Roman doctors, Far East healers, and medicine men of the indigenous peoples of the Americas! Can you say you've ever heard one of them complain about aches and pains?"

"I can't say I've heard anything from any of them at all."

"Proves my point, exactly." The old man tapped his eyebrow with the handle of his cane and gestured to a bag that was on the counter. "Take a bag full of these over the course of a month and you'll feel right as rain again!"

"I'm not feeling too poorly right now, just a touch of rheumatism…"

"Then you can't go wrong with these 'cure-all pills'. They combine a blend of herbs and other natural ingredients. Everyone knows that herbs are good for you. This will cure your rheumatism, also headaches, boils, verrucae, the vapors, indigestion, nausea, depression, headaches, confusion, contusions, concussions, conniptions, constipation, not to mention the pox, heartburn, headaches, and bad breath."

"…I have bad breath?"

"No, but they taste like peppermint, you see."

"And did you say, 'headaches' more than once?"

"The list of maladies this will cure is so long that I'm not surprised you wouldn't be able to keep them straight."

"I'm just not convinced that this sort of thing works."

"Of course they do, each one contains one-hundred percent natural—boy?" Mr. Mortenson spluttered, having noticed me.

"It contains 'boy'?" gasped Mr. Graham.

"No, the lad who just came in, there. He's—"

"Mr. Mortenson's assistant!" I interrupted.

The old man's beard poofed like a cat's tail as he stammered, "What!? No, that's—"

"Ah, splendid!" Mr. Graham said. "I didn't know you had hired on help."

"That's right!" I announced before he could object. "And you were about to describe the active ingredients that go into these here medicines, weren't you, Mr.

Mortenson, sir?"

I took the pouch from him and read the list of ingredients on its tag while he was still flabbergasted. The reader will remember that I had voraciously read and re-read all of the books in the Shroud's Creek schoolhouse, and luckily, one of those had been a field guide of natural remedies.

I explained, "Y'see, Mr. Graham, these pills contain turmeric, ginger root, and peppermint. Turmeric is a nat'ral painkiller. Ginger root has been used for centuries as a cure for all sorts o' digestive problems. And peppermint, well, that just tastes nice."

Mortenson was livid at the gumption I had shown, but the customer smiled and took the pouch into his hand.

"You've got a friendly disposition and an impressive knowledge there, son," he beamed. "Not to mention an accent. Where are you from?"

I answered, "Tennessee, sir. Born and bred. We know all about these things down there."

"I've never been, but I guess you'd know better than I."

"Sure enough, sir. Everyone knows that the further away things come from, the better they are. Just like mama used to say." At this point I was overdoing the southern charm, but you can't argue with results, can you?

"Top drawer! I say, you've convinced me. I'll take it."

"Superb. And can I also interest you in..." I took a swift glance around and settled on the flock of feathered woven bands which were hanging from the ceiling. I pulled one down and held it out in front of Mr. Graham. "...One of these?"

"Pardon my ignorance, but what is it?" he asked.

As to not betray my own ignorance on the object, I volleyed the question to the old man. "Why don't you tell him about it, Mr. Mortenson, sir?"

His expression had shifted from sheer fury to mild amusement. Leaning against a shelf with his arms crossed, he answered, "It's an Ojibwe dreamcatcher. It stops nightmares and encourages sound, restful sleep."

"And it's the gen-yoo-wine thing, too, ain't it?"

"As genuine as they come."

Mr. Graham, beaming with the wisdom of his selections, said, "That sounds fine, too. Ring, me up, young mister...?"

"Shuck, sir. Gunnar Shuck. It'd be my pleasure."

I walked to the register with the customer. Ysabel had been watching me with fascination, but scampered away when I went behind the counter, popping up again on another shelf so that she could observe from the safe distance of the other side of the room.

"So that's one-forty-nine for the cure-all, plus seventy-five cents for the dreamcatcher. Add the sales tax, and your total is two dollars and thirty-seven cents."

"Wow, I can't do math that quickly in *my* head," remarked Mr. Graham (no doubt truthfully) handing me a five-dollar bill.

"And your change is two-sixty-three," I said, handing him the cash and a fortune cookie. "And, here, take a complementary fortune cookie, all the way from... very far away."

"Wow! I'm becoming so worldly today." He cracked open the cookie and read his future. "*A NEW LOVE WILL ENTER YOUR LIFE SOON.* You don't say? I hope there's some way to change my fate. My wife would surely have a conniption if that happened. But wait, I just bought a cure for that! Funny how things work out. Good afternoon, gentlemen."

"Thank you kindly, Mr. Graham!" I called after him as he pushed through the doorway.

Mortenson added, "Give my regards to Anna, won't you? And why don't you pay a visit to Tumble's next door? Best to attack rheumatism with multiple remedies, I say."

The door closed, and I turned to the old man with a triumphant smile. He, however, held a far darker expression on his face, and he slowly aimed it at me.

A hiccup would be akin to cannon fire in the silence that followed.

Chapter 18

After the customer had left and I was alone with the old man, we stood staring at each in uncomfortable silence. The look in his old, milky eyes was conflicted, combining hesitation, pride, and consternation. Ysabel crept up and looked back and forth between us with anticipation. I decided to break the silence.

"So, that was a fine sale, wasn't it, sir?" I offered.

"Stubborn! Foolish! Indefatigable!" The old man huffed and puffed, along with several other words I didn't know the meanings of.

"Oh, come on. If I hadn't stepped in there, you woulda lost that sale."

"I would not have. I was whittling him down. He would have eventually given up."

"Even if that's true, because of me, that customer bought more than you would have convinced him to, and he left happy."

He sighed and answered, "I'll admit that I was impressed by that. You handled that customer very shrewdly. The part about the dreamcatcher being genuine was especially crafty—*heh heh*—considering I hand craft them myself."

"You said they *were* genuine."

"I said they were 'genuine as they come'. No one else around here makes them. I learned to make them from an Ojibwe craftsman I met up near Lake Superior. So, what I said was technically the truth."

"Do these things actually work, Mr. Mortenson?"

"Generally, yes. It's just that sometimes the most important ingredient for a medicine to work is the belief that it will."

"So that's why you told him to go next door and also buy medicine from Mr. Tumble?"

"Correct. That's called plausible deniability."

"You've made me a liar!"

"I didn't make you do anything, boy! You said what you had to in order to close the sale. You'll learn in time all that salesmanship comes down to is just creative lying. We've done nothing wrong. The customer gets his medicine and will feel better, and both Mr. Tumble and I make a profit. All benefit and none are harmed."

"In time? Does that mean you're going to let me work here?"

"I didn't say anything of the sort."

"You'd be a right fool not to take me up on this. I could help you increase your profits seven, maybe tenfold."

Stabbing the ground with his cane, Mortenson growled, "You're a stubborn young man. Head as hard as diamond. I can see that you aren't going to be deterred no matter what I say to you. It's particularly frustrating, because you remind me of another headstrong young man who didn't know when to quit."

"Who's that?"

"Me. Yours truly was also a hard-headed boy who stuck his nose in where it wasn't welcome and got himself into a whole lot of trouble for it. I was taller though. So, yes, Gunnar, you can work for me. Truth be told, there are some things that have become a struggle for me in my advanced age. Against my reason, I'll hire you as a shop assistant."

"Whoopee!" I hollered. "You won't regret this, Mr. Mortenson."

"Maybe I won't, but perhaps you will. Now that you're officially under my supervision, you're going to take orders from me, boy! Working here isn't always fun. It's not all magic and snipe hunts. Sometimes, we have to get our hands dirty and put ourselves in the way of real danger. Death, dismemberment, disgruntled clients, and even worse can happen to you here. These are the risks all retail employees face. I'll start you at a dollar a day. Do you accept that?"

"Yes, I do, sir!"

The old man wrinkled his mustache into a smug grin and softly uttered, "You say that now, but I'll wager that by the end of the day, that enthusiasm of yours will be drained away, and you'll never want to step foot in another Curiosity Shop again. Mark my words, lad. There are things far more sinister and deadly out there than squonks and not-deer. I've encountered many things in my life that could easily kill you, or worse. Some of them are locked away right now in my storeroom. As a matter of fact..."

Mr. Mortenson hobbled to the door at the back of the store, and pulled out his ancient, iron key.

"Come with me, and I'll show you where you'll be doing most of your work."

The moment was finally here. I could almost taste the answers to all my questions before me as the old man inserted the key into the lock. My heart began to beat with percussive force strong enough to beat down the door itself. Mortenson turned the key, opened the door, and welcomed me into his storeroom.

Chapter 19

As Mortenson opened the door to the storeroom, I realized that there was a pattern to my interactions with this old man. Every time I delved into the secrets of the magical Curiosity Shop and thought I had hit bedrock, entirely new depths of mystery were revealed to me.

I was like Sisyphus, repeatedly trying to push a boulder to the top of a mountain, only for it to tumble back to the bottom where I would have to start again. My boulder, however, sold aromatic candles and dubious remedies. Every mystery box opened to reveal another, and another, and more still.

This was what went through my head when I first entered the storeroom at the back of the Curiosity Shop.

Hundreds of literal mystery boxes presented themselves when Mr. Mortenson opened the door, and I stepped through. Crates stacked on shelves that reached all the way to the two-story high ceiling. These shelves also stretched all the way back to… well… There was no visible end to the room.

The walls and shelves went on and on, perspective shrinking them together as they raced on into infinity. Gravity itself seemed to be drawn into this unknowable expanse. I felt vertigo as I stared—down?—as if I were hovering over a bottomless abyss, even though I was securely on the ground. I'd seen the back side of the shop from outside. There's no way this room could be longer on the inside than it was outside.

Mr. Mortenson noticed my eyes had widened and legs became shaky, and chuckled, "You look as if you're going to be sick, my boy. You've never been in a magically augmented space before, I take it? Not too many of those in Okabedokee?"

"I told you, I'm from... *urgh*..."

"Your eyes and stomach aren't deceiving you, lad. Inside, it looks like a normal room with right-angled corners and straight walls, but if you could see it from outside you would see that the volume of this room is folded in on itself like an accordion. By this method I can fit a room into a container that is much smaller than itself. It takes the senses some getting used to, hmm?"

My senses *were* rejecting what they were presented with in this storeroom. The walls, floor, and ceiling were bathed in an orange light which had no apparent source, as if it was always coming from behind me, no matter which way I faced. The air smelled like static electricity. I heard the sound of a machine humming, although it didn't enter my ears. It felt as though it were projected directly into my brain.

"Take a minute to orient yourself," Mortenson said.

"I'm fine," I lied. "Just need to catch my breath."

I put my hands on my waist, doubled over, and took in a deep breath. A tingling sensation filled my lungs, which then passed on to my stomach as a nausea.

"You won't want to breathe too deeply in here, boy. The air is saturated with magic. Take in too much, and anything could happen. Don't want you changing shape on us."

"Like Mr. Tumble's pet next door?" I challenged him, still trying to fight back the urge to vomit.

"Tumble? I wasn't aware that he had a pet at all."

"How could you miss it? He has an animal that changes species every night or so. It's been an elephant before, for Pete's sake!"

"I see. Are you sure he's not an exotic animal collector?"

I lifted my head to say *Bless Your Heart* to him with my eyes.

"Okay, okay," he conceded. "It's hard to imagine that's caused by anything *other* than magic spilling over from my shop. Probably caused by a leak somewhere in the cracks of the mortar. I'm going to have to take a close look around to find it and stop the poor beast's suffering. Did the druggist seem upset about it when you spoke to him?"

"The critter itself seems to be fine, and Mr. Tumble has gotten used to it."

"Oh, marvelous. He mustn't suspect me, then. In that case, there's no rush."

I began to straighten my back and asked, "So magic *is* real? What is it, exactly? How does it work?"

Mortenson considered this question, then stammered, "Magic is... well... magic."

"That ain't no kinda answer! If you can use it to make a room bigger on the inside than the outside, then surely you know how it works."

"I have some knowledge of the practical application of magic, but I haven't quite figured out the exact science of it. The best I can do to explain it is that it is a form of energy—like electricity—but with a will of its own. What it desires is form, flesh. It finds it by peering into the hearts and minds of human beings, taking our dreams, beliefs, wishes, and even fears and manifesting them. In all honesty, though, this is only a working theory.

"The one thing I do know for certain is that magic is very dangerous to meddle with. Anyone can use magic who knows how, as well as any creatures created *with* magic. In the hands of someone who wanted to do harm, they could do a great deal of it indeed. Luckily, I'm just using it to make more storage space, so the ill effects *should* be minimal, unless being surrounded by magic makes you feel ill. Are you allergic to magic? Hoho!"

I only glared sarcastically at the old man, and once I had collected myself (and held down my lunch), he started to close the door. Before he could, however, Ysabel appeared from seemingly nowhere to block the doorway with her body, as is standard practice for her species. She glared suspiciously at me.

Mortenson stopped just short of flattening the tiny black cat and shouted, "Aargh! Don't do that! What do you want?"

She continued to stare angrily at me.

"The boy works here now, Ysabel. He'll be fine."

"...Meow," she said.

"Oh, come off it. I know what I said the other day, but I think he's trustworthy. You can supervise him if it will satisfy you."

Ysabel still refused to budge.

"Well? Are you coming in or not?"

She finally made up her mind and sauntered into the storeroom. Her fur stood up on end momentarily as she entered the magic field. The old man mumbled a curse at the cat under his breath and locked the door behind her. She merely flicked the end of her tail at him.

Now that all were present and accounted for, we could delve deeper into the storeroom.

Chapter 20

THE SHELVES AT THE front of the storeroom contained a variety of bizarre artifacts, some in wooden boxes, some in glass display cases, and others lying naked, gathering dust on the shelf. Looking around at the plethora of alien objects, one particularly interesting thing caught my eye.

In a small glass jar, seated comfortably on a stone and surrounded by water was a small, warty, brown toad. Its eyes were shut, and it did not appear to be breathing. I could not tell if this tiny creature was merely sleeping, or even alive.

"Step back from that, boy!" Mortenson suddenly barked at me.

"Why?" I asked, startled. "Is it dangerous?"

"Not in his current state of dormancy, but you could do a great deal of harm to him if you wake him up. I would just prefer that you don't disturb the wee thing's rest. He's had a long century."

Some things are too strange for even my mind to digest all at once, so I decided to leave this amphibious mystery alone and turned my attention to another noteworthy item nearby.

It was like a human hand, with four slender digits and a thumb. Three of these were extended, and the thumb and pinky curled in to meet. Unlike a human hand, however, it was much smaller, furry, and the palm was covered in dark, leathery skin. It was held up in a wood and glass display case on a wire stand.

"What about this one? Is it a... a... Peruvian shrunken back scratcher?" I joked.

"Very funny lad, but no. What you see before you is none other than a monkey's paw."

"I ain't never heard of one of these coming without the whole monkey, so I'll assume that it's magical, somehow. It's kinda gross..."

In response to this comment, the monkey's paw shifted its fingers to make an obscene gesture at me.

"Now, now," Mortenson shushed. "The boy is new to all this. Don't take what he says personally. I'm sure you'll get along before long."

As it curled itself into a fist, I cringed. "Yuck... Is it dangerous?"

"Aye, potentially. A monkey's paw will grant three wishes to whoever holds it, but at a cost. Every wish that it grants will go horribly wrong, manifesting as more of a curse."

"Have you made a wish on it, sir?"

"How do you think I determined that I had a genuine monkey's paw? Yes, I made a wish on it, one I thought couldn't possibly backfire, but oh—I have paid dearly for it. Now I keep it locked away in here so that no one else can be tempted."

"What did you wish for?"

Mortenson picked the trailing half of his beard off the floor and sighed, "I wished to get my long, handsome hair back."

I thought I heard Ysabel snicker but chalked that up to my imagination.

"What if you made a wish on it that changed the way it worked, so that the wishes didn't go wrong?" I asked.

Mortenson's eyes went blank as he considered this. "The monkey's paw is an incredibly litigious object. The wording would need to be very precise to make it work. I should write something up and run it by Mr. Hammeboerger or Freiss to review it for legal loopholes. I may need to return to experiment on this in the future..." he muttered something under his breath before waving the thought away and moving on.

The three of us ventured deeper into the storeroom, past shelves full to the brim with wooden crates. Many of them were held in place by chains, surrounded by salt, or both. One was partly submerged in a washbasin filled with a blurry, pink liquid. Every box was labelled not with a name, but a serial number, and designated with a marker that read CAT1, CAT2, or CAT3.

Passing by one of the CAT3 boxes, it suddenly began to shake violently, rattling its chains as it tried to lunge at me. The usual options of fight or flight were presented to me, and it took me no time at all to judge what my chances would be against this unknown monster in a tussle. I leapt backward with a "YEEP!" and caught myself on the opposite shelf.

Mr. Mortenson, who hadn't so much as raised an eyebrow in surprise, whacked the aggressive container with his cane and yelled, "Hey, you! Stop that this instant! Try as you might, you'll never get out of there, so long as I'm standing. I beat you once, and I could always do it again!"

The box returned to its dormant state, and sensing the danger had passed, I pulled myself upright. I realized that in my panic, I had cowered against another crate, which vibrated angrily when I touched it.

"Aigh!" I yelped as I jumped away from it. "What in TARnation is in these things?"

"Monsters, lad," Mortenson answered. "Each one captured and contained so they can't do any more harm. This is at the heart of what I do here. I capture dangerous creatures and artifacts and store them away.

"Each one gets a serial number and a category, based on how dangerous they are. A CAT1 is capable of causing serious disruption, chaos, or otherwise unpleasant hijinks. CAT2 is for the creatures that can and/or will kill. The final category, CAT3, is for those monsters who will do so much worse than that."

"Worse? What's worse than killin'?"

"I shudder to think about it. Pray you never have to face down a CAT3, son."

"Okay, but how do you keep track of them? Why don't you just write the name of the creature on them?"

"I keep the identities of these beasts a secret in the extreme event that unwanted eyes come snooping in here. No one ever has, but I won't take any chances in case it ever does happen. There is an inventory list I use to match the serial numbers to the identities of each creature, and that is stashed away in a magically locked safe. Only I have access to it."

"What about this one, here? What category is he?" I asked, approaching a creature that was sitting by itself in a big glass jar, snacking on a ball of mozzarella. It was hunched over, fuzzy, horribly ugly, and sniffling over its meal. I recognized it then with no mistake.

"Oh, it's the squonk. Hello, there!" I greeted it. The poor creature squealed and twisted in shock to stare at me, and immediately broke into hysterics. It went transparent and with a *sloosh*, dissolved once more into a pool of tears, leaving nothing behind but some very soggy cheese. Ysabel curiously sniffed the jar and then hissed at it.

"Oops, sorry," I apologized as the squonk bubbled in frustration.

"The squonk doesn't fall into any of the categories. It can be a pest but is ultimately harmless. Don't worry, little fellow," Mortenson cooed, patting the jar. "Once I figure out where your nest is I'll return you to the woods. Until then, I'll make sure you have enough cheese to satisfy you. Would you like to try some parmesan next?"

This seemed to pacify the puddle, and it quit bubbling.

I thought I understood the meaning of the old man having shown me all this, and asked, "Is this what you want me to do back here, then? Watch over these here critters and look after them? Or maybe we have to destroy the dangerous ones through some kind of hocus pocus, or occult whatchamacallit?"

"Well, yes, the storage and upkeep of these beasts is an important part of our work here," answered Mortenson. "What I need you to do—what you'll be spending the bulk of your time on—is at this desk over here."

Chapter 21

Mortenson led me to a writing desk against the eastern wall, which was flanked on both sides by bookshelves. The shelf on the right-hand side had hundreds of ledgers, so many that the ones on the higher shelf were far above my head. On the left-hand side were a collection of ancient tomes and manuscripts, some yellowed scrolls of parchment and others bound in leather, with titles such as *Creatures and Beasts of Legende and Mythe* and *Demonology for the Lay Man*.

The desk was ornamented by a single candlestick, a feather pen and inkwell, and a tiny painted figurine of a cat with one paw raised and a large coin in the other. If nothing else made me wary of the old man up to this point, I should have practiced more caution on discovering that he was a cat person. Once you own both a cat and cat-themed merchandise, you are far beyond hope.

The old man pulled out the chair and seated me down at the desk. He strummed his finger over the ledgers, removed one labelled '1901,' and slapped it down in front of me.

"Here's what I need you to do, Gunnar," he said. "Lately, I've been having trouble balancing the end-of-year ledger, and you seem to have a gift for figures and a sharp young mind, so you'll spend this afternoon balancing this and making sure we meet the minimum balance that I've written here."

He pointed to the desired sum at the top of the page,

and my jaw nearly slammed on the table when I saw what was owed. *That* much, and due... tonight!? The scratched-out sums Mortenson had attempted on the following pages were not the only thing here that didn't add up.

"End o' the year?" I asked. "We're only at the end o' August. Tax season don't start 'til March."

Suddenly, the old man's demeanor shifted, becoming dark and foreboding. Ominously, he answered, "This isn't taxes. Someone is coming tonight—at midnight—to collect their yearly dues."

"Someone is comin'? Who?"

"The one who is coming tonight is the... er... the Landlord, let's call him. He's coming to collect the... rent."

This was no explanation at all, so I pressed him further. "I'm brighter'n I might seem, Mr. Mortenson, and I can tell you're fibbin' me."

"I'm not lying to you, except perhaps by omission. Don't ask questions you aren't prepared for, boy. That's an important lesson that you should learn the easy way, by listening to me, instead of the hard way, which is how I learned it."

"I'm not afraid of anything, Mr. Mortenson, least of all a debt collector."

"Have you ever had to deal with one? If you had, you might reconsider."

"What kind of landlord demands a huge payment like this, all at once, at midnight one night every year?"

"The kind who—if not paid at the appointed time in full—will visit serious and deadly consequences for it. I appreciate that you are my assistant now, and I'll inform you on matters when and where they become appropriate, but this is one that I cannot allow you to know about. *Ever.* You would wish you *didn't* know if you did. All you need to concern yourself with is balancing this year's ledger and letting me know if our assets meet the fee or not. Have I made myself clear?"

I knew then that I had pressed the old man to the limits of how far he was willing to go. He was up against the cliff's edge, and he would rather plummet than give in to my demands for answers any longer. Before, he treated me and my inquiries with caution, but now I had reached a point he would never budge on.

There was no key for this door; he had swallowed it.

I wasn't going to get any more answers from him now, so I decided I ought to relent for now. Perhaps there would be a way to learn more from him later.

"Yes, sir," I answered. "Clear as a bell. I'll get right to work on the ledger, and I'll let y' know what the balance comes out to."

"Very good," he said grimly, then turned to the cat. "Ysabel, stay here and supervise. Make sure the lad does his job and does it right."

"Meow," said Ysabel, and she climbed up to the top of the shelf that loomed over the desk. She hung her head and both paws over the edge and stared at me with unblinking yellow eyes.

"I'll be back in an hour or so to check on your progress. Until then, attend to your work, and don't you dare touch anything, if for no one else's sake but your own," the old man warned, and then disappeared into the darkness at the entrance to the store room. I heard a distant clanking of the door, and then knew that I was alone with my feline supervisor.

"I don't s'pose you could fill me in on what this is all about?" I asked her, but she merely laid down on her paws, yawned, and then dozed off to sleep.

"Whelp, that's just peachy," I moaned, dipping my pen into the inkwell, and setting about calculating the balance of the ledger.

Chapter 22

The work of balancing the ledger proved to be harder than I expected. The basic task of performing sums was the easy part; what I had not been prepared for was the soul-draining monotony of it.

Hunched over a badly lit desk, I strained myself to keep working. My wrists, back, eyes, and *brain* ached from doing this dull work. It was meaningless, only for some vague benefit, none of which had anything to do with me. I longed to do some other, *any* other task, such as mucking out a monster cage, if only for some break in my boredom. Was this all that office work was?

It was like watching paint dry... in the can.

Occasionally, I would stare up at Ysabel snoozing on the shelf above me. She had not so much as turned over in all the time I was working. When I had begun, I regarded her as cute, pleasant company. However, as time passed and her leisure became more and more contrasted with my labor, my feelings for her slowly morphed into jealousy, and eventually, blind hatred. As it goes with cats, so too does it go with supervisors, and double if they are one in the same body.

Hopefully, advancements made in the coming century, whether social, economic, or technological, could make this kind of work a thing of the past.

Even in a task as dull as this, however, the unusual nature of the magical Curiosity Shop carried over and created jarring distinctions.

For example, I had expected the assets to be listed in cash, and to be sure, most of them were represented by bills and coins obtained from sales. Likewise, expenditures were always represented in simple American dollar amounts. However, there were plenty of assets listed in terms of precious jewels, metals, or what can only be described as "other".

Gold dollar coins are commonly used in American transactions, but there were a number of coins listed in exotic denominations. This included a sack full of Roman dineri, Judean silver, and... Spanish doubloons? As in pirate's gold? Mr. Mortenson didn't strike me as the swashbuckling type, so I had to believe that he wasn't involved in piracy. I couldn't help but entertain the remote possibility, however, and that led my mind on a tangent where I considered possible pirate names for the old man, such as "Levi Longbeard" and "Ol' Gray Mort".

The mind goes to some strange places when crushed under the weight of boredom.

There were also a number of Japanese Koban listed with a note that said *'Highly adulterated with aluminum and other worthless metals. Do not waste time seeking these out in the future.'*

One listed asset was, and I quote, a "cursed tiara". The object had been itemized in the ledger by its components, consisting of thirty small diamonds, eleven "walnut-sized" emeralds, four rubies, a solid silver headband, and one large blue diamond. The total value was estimated at $2,780, which seemed low until I remembered the five Cs of diamond valuation. These are Cut, Color, Clarity, Carat, and Curse.

Another entry was for a solid golden idol of unknown origin. Mortenson had entertained himself by speculating on the purpose of the figure:

Appears to be goddess figure with many eyes, mouths, and noses. Matches no description of any known folkloric deity. Possibly belonging to heretofore undiscovered civilization. Warrants further research. Spiritual value is not *taken into consideration. Estimated value: $150*

There was one entry in the list of sales which particularly drew my attention. On February the 22nd this year, Mortenson notes that he sold a crystal fortune telling ball, a guide to runic symbology, and a starter kit of mystic candles to...

Shannon Hollinger.

So, my hunch had been correct. That occult setup of my aunt's that I had discovered hidden in the walls of our house had all been obtained here. This made me wonder; why would someone as secretive and cautious as Mortenson sell something as potentially dangerous as a future-peering crystal ball to anyone? He barely trusted me to balance his books and locked all of the actual magical artifacts in the back of his shop. Perhaps the old man knew her well enough to trust her? Did they have some kind of close, personal relationship? Maybe... possibly... they were... Ugh, no.

Thoughts like that are best wrapped up in a sack, tied to a heavy stone, and tossed into the river.

If she had purchased a fortune telling ball here and it indeed worked, then what future event was she trying to predict? I began to grow worried. Was she trying to see how she would die? Was she worried that some disaster would befall her, or even the whole town? There were a number of fearsome objects and creatures locked up in here, perhaps she was aware of something about Mortenson's collection that worried her?

The crystal had a big crack running through it when I discovered it. This suggested that whatever my aunt saw caused her to become violently upset. I realized that I was letting my mind run amuck with feverish speculation and tried to calm myself down to refocus on my work. Dangerous or not, I was going to have to ask the old man for some answers, and this time, I wouldn't back down until I got them.

Despite the spinning frenzy that my mind had gotten into, I managed to finish calculating the balance of

Mortenson's 1901 assets and found that they fell just short of his goal. I double, triple, and quadruple checked the figures. Pretty close, but not quite there. He wouldn't be happy about this.

I closed the ledger and carried it to the bookshelf to replace it. The lower shelf had books for dates going back to... the 1730's? How old was this place, exactly? Never mind, I had to put this back in its place.

The newer books were on a higher shelf. Curse my lack of height! I couldn't reach it, even if I stood on the chair that had spent the past hour and a half chafing my backside. It couldn't possibly matter that much where I put it, I figured, so I decided I would just set it on a shelf that I could reach.

"Mreow!" snarled Ysabel suddenly as I was about to set the ledger down. She had been so silent the entire time, I had completely forgotten about her. Now she was leaning over and glaring at me angrily with her teeth bared and her back arched.

"What's eatin' you, kitty?" I said out loud, turning away from her and trying to set the book down again.

She interrupted me again with a *HISSSSSSS!*

"What? I'm putting the book down, no reason to get upset."

Once more, I tried to set down the ledger on the convenient shelf, but this time I was startled by an unfamiliar voice.

"Oh, for heaven's sake!" Ysabel shouted. "Do I have to do everything myself!?"

Chapter 23

I JUMPED AT THIS unexpected exclamation from the cat, even though I thought I was prepared for anything at this point.

"Cripes!" I yelped. "You can talk?"

The black cat gracefully hopped down from the high shelf to one at my eye level. "Of course, I can talk, foolish human!" she snapped, as if I had said something extraordinarily stupid.

"You didn't before, or wait… I think I know what's goin' on here. The air in this place is magically charged. That must be why you can speak in here."

The angry look she gave me would paralyze even Ms. Pearson. "How rude! I don't require magic to talk. Do you?"

"Well, no, but see… I'm human."

"I suppose you think that makes you soooo clever. I've seen a great many humans without half the brains I have, and even they speak without magic, although that would be the only explanation for how they obtained the ability."

"I'm sorry, I didn't mean to insult you," I said, realizing subconsciously that I was trying to be diplomatic with a cat. "It's just that you didn't talk before, and I didn't assume you could."

"It wasn't worth the effort to talk to you until just now. Just because someone chooses to be silent doesn't mean they are mute. Some of us speak only when we have something to say, instead of filling the air with meaningless noise as you humans like to do so much."

"So, can *all* cats talk then?"

"No," she answered, calming down. "As a matter of fact, only black cats can talk. Think of all the talking cats you've met, and you'll realize that every one of them was a black cat."

"I've never met a single other talkin' cat."

"Oh. Well, if you had, you'd know that only black cats can talk. And even then, only if they feel like it. We can't go wasting precious breath for anything that isn't worthy of it."

"Apparently my puttin' the book on the wrong shelf was worth it."

"Yes, it was. If you're going to do something, then do it right."

"You didn't say anything when I was balancin' the books. As a matter of fact, you weren't even watchin' then."

"You didn't make any mistakes then—by some miracle—and I didn't have to look to know that. All cats, talking and non-talking, possess the ability to tell when things are incorrect at any given time."

"I can't reach the shelf, in case you couldn't see from all the way up in your nappin'—I'm sorry, your supervisin' spot."

"Ugh, don't you know anything? You don't have to reach the shelf, just tell the book to return to its place."

I could only reply to this statement from Ysabel with an incredulous stare.

"Go on," she said. "Try it."

I figured that if I was arguing with a cat, then commanding a book wouldn't be much more of a stretch. I held it out in front of me, then gave one more glance at Ysabel to try and see through her poker face. This, of course, is impossible. It's a good thing that cats cannot hold cards, otherwise they would bluff their way to total economic dominance. I sighed and gave my order to the book.

"Book, return to your place on the shelf."

Suddenly, the book vibrated, wobbling with increasing ferocity until I lost my grip on it. It stuck the landing, righting itself on a pair of wooden legs that had magically sprouted from the spine. It trotted over to the base of the shelf on feet like wooden clogs that went *clop, clop, clop*. It crouched, wiggled its spine, and jumped all the way to the high shelf, sliding into its place next to the 1900 ledger. The legs retracted back into the spine and disappeared without a trace.

The cat and I gazed back at one another, me with amazement, and her with smug satisfaction.

"See, wasn't that easy?" she sneered. "I swear, if I weren't the manager of this shop, nothing would ever get done."

I rolled my eyes and replied, "The *manager*, you say? What about Mr. Mortenson?"

"Oh, *technically* it's Levi's shop. But really, I'm the one in charge here."

"You don't think you'd be more at home in a... a witch's hut or somethin', instead of a Curiosity Shop?"

"No, no-no-no. Witches are far too bossy. Around here, I can do what I please because as I've said, *I'm* the boss."

"Witches are real, too? No, that's a stupid thing to say, of course they are."

"I've met a few cats who've lived with a witch, and trust me, it's far more work than a cat is meant for. I've got my paws tied up around here as it is, supervising, you see."

"A supervisor who is paid in sardines, huh?"

"You don't have any on you right now, do you?" she asked, suddenly sweetening up. "I may be in charge but I'm not above taking a bribe."

"No, I ain't got any fish on me."

"Pity. I'll do most anything for fresh fish."

This gave me an idea. "I could always get some for ya," I offered. "I just wanna ask you some questions first."

"Hmm, seems like a fair trade. I'll answer three questions, and then you have to get me some fish. What do you want to know?"

I thought for a second. What could I assume the cat would know about Mortenson's operations? Possibly everything, come to think of it. I decided to take my chances with a hardball line of questioning.

"What does Mortenson do with the creatures and artifacts that are kept back here?" I asked.

She scowled and me and answered, "You're going to waste your first question on something you can plainly see for yourself?"

"You mean he just keeps 'em here? A businessman as shrewd as him doesn't try to do nothin' with these potentially valuable specimens?"

"Potentially valuable, yes, but *definitely* dangerous. Levi has been catching these things for a long time, and trust me, as much as he loves to turn a quick buck, he'd never let a single one of them free again. No chance."

"How long has he been doing this?"

This question was apparently a touchy one for the cat, because she paused before muttering, "...A long, *long* time."

"Okay, fair enough. One more question. Who is this so-called Landlord? He sure demands a lot of money for rent. You have to agree that it's pretty strange for a landlord to collect a sum like that on only one night a year at midnight."

Ysabel considered this question, placing a paw under her chin, and then licked it before answering, "I can show you the answer to that one, but I'll need you to help me," she replied ominously.

"Help you? With what?"

"I need you to open something for me. You may have noticed that I don't have any thumbs. If I have to give you humans one thing, it's the invention of thumbs. Do this for me, then all of the answers to your questions will be revealed."

CHAPTER 24

YSABEL DIDN'T WAIT FOR me to agree, she just trotted off toward the deeper recesses of the storeroom. I paused, suspicious of the sudden serpent-tongued turn the cat had taken. Something was off, and I wasn't entirely sure that I should trust her. Who knows what kind of Faustian deal this feline might be trying to trick me into?

"Come on, don't dilly-dally," she called. "You want to know the answers, don't you?"

I decided to follow her, keeping a skeptical mindset.

The deeper we went into the storeroom, the more saturated the atmosphere became with magic. My vision, which had been aided by an orange light whose source I couldn't find, was starting to shift into colors I had never seen before and seemed impossible. Blues, violets, and greens appeared to blend into colors that I had never before experienced.

The static tingling sensation of each breath I drew steadily intensified, and the hairs on my arm stood straight up. I had to stop several times to compose myself and adjust to the increasing magical pressure as Ysabel scoffed at me.

"Tsk, tsk, tsk. At this rate, he'll never find the answers," she teased. "Would you like to turn back, little human?"

"I'm fine, thank you kindly!" I gasped.

"Well, then, come on. We're almost there."

I caught up to the cat, who was perched on top of a crate. It was unlabeled and held shut with iron nails. At this point, the light had ceased to resemble color any longer. Everything appeared to be glossy black. It was no longer like real light, but some kind of inverted darkness.

"This is it; I just need you to open this box, and everything will be revealed." Ysabel said.

"Open it with what?" I panted.

"There's a crowbar behind you," she said, leaping across to the shelf where indeed, the tool was lying. "Just open that box. Quickly, now."

I was panting and sweating from the oppressive magical atmosphere, but I still had my wits about me, and wasn't about to open something without knowing what was inside of it.

"Tell me what's in there," I demanded.

"You just have to see it for yourself. It's Mortenson's little secret," Ysabel replied with a lick of the lips.

"All of these other crates hold some kinda eldritch monster or unspeakable terror. How do I know I'm not openin' Pandora's Box 'r somethin'?"

"Come on, now. I'd never ask you to unleash something horrible like that. You can trust me. The answers are right there in front of you. You just have to open it."

The temptation proved to be too great for me. I grabbed the crowbar and held it up in the… not exactly light, but whatever unnatural force granted me sight this deep in the storeroom.

"There's nothin' evil in there, you swear?" I asked the cat, who was hopping with excitement.

"Quite the opposite. It's something wonderful. Do it!"

I steadied myself in front of the crate, raised my tool, and prepared to plunge it under the lid to pry it loose. As I was driving it down, however, I was stopped by the appearance of a ghoulish figure.

"Stop that, this instant!" cried a familiar gravelly voice. "Don't open that!"

It was Mr. Mortenson, appearing nightmarish in the dark light, frantically swinging his cane.

"M-Mr. Mortenson, s-sir!" I blubbered. "I'm sorry, I

didn't know! Ysabel tricked me!"

"MREOW! Snitch!" she hissed.

"Go on, naughty cat! Get out of here!" the old man exclaimed, shooing her away with his cane. The cat yowled and scampered away into parts unseen.

"It's a good thing I got here when I did," Mortenson scolded.

I dropped to my knees and begged, "Forgive me, sir! I have no idea what kind of horrible evil I might have unleashed."

"Hmm?" he responded. "Horrible evil? What, now? Oh, hah. No, I'm afraid not, boy. Ysabel knows better than to open the crates that actually have something dangerous in them."

"Then... what was in that crate?"

"Salted herring. Hoho!"

My shoulders sagged. "Wha... that's it?"

"Well, it means a great deal to her. They're her favorite snack, and I was hiding them here so she wouldn't steal them when I wasn't looking. She figured out where they were and was trying to trick you into giving them to her."

I was beside myself, slumped and deflated on the floor.

"Hoho," laughed the old man. "Looks like you're all the worse for wear in this stuffy magical air. What say you we go back to the desk where it's not so uncomfortable?"

Mortenson hoisted me up under the arms and helped me to my feet, and then walked me back to the front of the storeroom where the desk was. My vision and breathing returned to normal, or at least more normal, and I was finally able to support myself.

"I'm sorry about what happened, sir. I won't let that cat fool me again," I apologized.

"Oh, don't worry about that," the old man answered. "You couldn't have done any real harm in here with a measly crowbar. If you had meant to do anything truly nefarious, Ysabel would have stopped you. She really got your goat though, hmm?"

"I didn't make it easy for her, though."

"Absolutely," he replied with a glib smile. "If that makes you feel better. Now, let's see the work you've done. 1901 ledger, come to me!"

The book high on the shelf sprouted a pair of wooden legs once again. It wriggled them in the air for a moment while it gained its bearings, then coiled up, and launched itself into his hands. He opened it, ran a finger over the figures I had run, and then scratched his chin and brought his eyebrows together.

"Oh, bother," he lamented. "This won't do. We're short and the total is due at midnight, only four hours away."

I suggested, "Maybe we could talk to the Landlord and he'd grant us an extension for a day or two? After all, we're only short by a small amount."

"No, the Landlord won't grant a microsecond more for want of even a single penny. It has to be exact, or he's going to... take me away. Then there won't be anyone to make sure these creatures stay locked up. It would be a disaster..."

"Is there any way to get the funds we're missing at this hour?"

"I was hoping I wouldn't have to resort to this, but as a matter of fact, there is. I'm afraid I'm going to have to ask you to work some overtime this evening. We're going to have to go into the woods."

"The woods? I've heard some rumors about them."

"Whatever you've heard, I assure you it's not even a fraction of the full story. There's no time to rest, though. We need to start moving. You must be hungry, though. While you were working, I prepared some sandwiches for you if you needed a break. Can't go on this errand on an empty stomach, so we'll eat them along the way."

"Oh, thank you, sir."

"Absolutely. Make sure you're dressed for a long hike. I can lend you a pair of boots if you need. Oh, and I'll show you where the tools are kept. We're going to need a lantern, some sacks and... two shovels."

Chapter 25

Precious reader, if your employer ever hands you a shovel and tells you to follow them out into the woods late in the dark of night, kindly inform them that, no thank you, you will be going home and will only return to collect the wages you are still owed. To my eternal shame, I did not make the sensible decision. I was a foolhardy fourteen-year-old boy, driven by curiosity, who chose to go along with this suspect errand.

My experience with forests was limited to those near Shroud's Creek, which I had ventured into many times with my friends when I was a little kid. We would stomp around in there catching bugs, climbing trees, and playing make-believe that we were adventurous explorers. Even at night, those woods felt safe, illuminated by the glow of lightning bugs, and the only thing we encountered there were skittish deer.

These woods had a very different atmosphere. The trees had crooked, twisting branches, and the soil underfoot crunched with dead leaves and pinecones. Deep shadows surrounded me, and the lantern I carried did little but make me feel like a glowing target. I felt totally exposed there. Combined with the rumors I had heard from Herbie, I felt as though anything might be lurking in the shadows, waiting to strike.

I was beginning to regret following the old man out here, but he appeared to have no cares in the world at all. He strolled along, happily swinging his cane with each step, his shovel slung over his other shoulder. He had wound his beard around his neck like a scarf so that it wouldn't drag on the ground. The end of it flapped against his back like a cape. If he had any fear at all, he did a marvelous job concealing it.

I, meanwhile, held my shovel close to my chest expecting to have to swing it at any moment, and gripped the lantern so tightly that my fingers went numb. Normally I was fearless in the face of the unknown, but this was on a whole other level.

"Mr. Mortenson, sir," I whispered when I could no longer stand the silence, "You must know what this looks like. What're we out here for?"

He didn't turn around, but continued to gallivant forward as he replied, "Fret not, lad. I assure you that this errand is nothing untoward. I'll explain the details to you when we get to our destination. We're heading toward the mountains, looking for a specific cliff in particular."

"I see. And what should I expect we'll be doin' when we get there?"

"Collecting something. We're most of the way there, already. Trust me, I've been through these woods many times and know my way, even in the dark."

"I've been in the dark, so to speak, even since I started workin' for you."

"Don't tell me you're nervous?"

"I already told you; I heard some rumors about these woods that I think—yes—are worthy of some concern."

"Rumors like what?"

"My friend at school said there was a witch in the woods. Is that true?"

"A witch? I've never met one, but don't worry, there are far worse things out there than witches."

"Don't worry? Oh, *Bless Yer Heart; yer so kind; thank ya.*"

"You say that a lot; it's very thoughtful of you."

"What kind o' critters can I expect to see out here?"

"Oh, the usual. Deer, bears, plenty of squirrels. Also a

few tribes of generally harmless fairy folk and other paranormal entities. These woods have a long and fascinating history of supernatural encounters and dangerous beasts. You're aware that before it was known as the United States of America, this land was made up of many nations of people? People who were here ages before any European dreamed that a western hemisphere even existed?"

"I know a little about that, but they don't talk much about it in school."

"Hmmph! That figures. See now, before they were forced off their land by European invaders, this was Lenape territory. They called this part of the woods 'The Devils' Forest'. It was a place where evil spirits thrived. They never came around here if they could help it."

"What kind of evil spirits are we talkin' about, here?"

"Back in those times, these woods were infested by man-killing monsters, like the wendigo. Terrifying creatures that could control the mind of a human and cause them to commit horrifying deeds. I hope I never cross paths with one of them ever again."

"And... those are lurkin' around here still?"

"Well, no, not as far as I've been able to find. If any still live in these woods, they are dormant, desperately hanging on for life."

"What happened to them?"

"Are you aware of the concept of an invasive species?"

"Vaguely. It means an animal or plant that moves from its home habitat to another one and causes trouble, right?"

"That's the basic idea, but it doesn't just apply to living organisms. See, when people move around, they bring their beliefs, folklore, and culture with them."

"So, when the Europeans came, they brought their mythical creatures and monsters with them. Is that what you're saying?"

"You hit the nail on the head. Unknown to the European immigrants, a small population of small pests snuck on board their ships, came with them, and settled in the new world. This happened with ordinary creatures like rats and insects, but also with folkloric ones. Instead of stowing away on a ship, however, these were carried in the minds and beliefs of the settlers.

"Once the Europeans reached this area and came into contact with the high concentration of magic in this forest, their worst fears and wildest dreams could take physical shape. Thus, the myths and legends became flesh. With no natural enemies, these foreign beings were able to thrive in their adopted habitat, to the detriment of the ones that were already here."

"Don't that mean that they won out by being the strongest? The most fit to survive?"

"That depends on what you mean by strength in this instance. If you define strength as the ability to win in a fair competition, or having the conviction to conduct oneself ethically, you will have a difficult time making that case. If you define it as underhanded cunning and an unsatisfiable hunger to win at any cost, you may be on the right track."

"But... ain't that a good thing?" I asked naively, which caused the old man to finally stop and look at me with concern. "I mean, if the wendigos and other monsters are gone, ain't that better?"

"A creature can't help its nature, even if that means you might be its prey," he replied solemnly. "And the human-devouring beasts weren't the only ones to suffer. These woods were once home to a plethora of benign fairy folk that dwelled among the trees and flowers, living harmoniously in the balance of their ecosystem. They're all gone from here now. No, the terror of the wendigo and the other native creatures is long over. They've been replaced by our own far more vicious monsters."

Mortenson, dark and brooding, turned from me then to continue the trek. I couldn't possibly return to the eerie ambience of the forest, not after *that* speech, so I filled the vacuum with the question, "Can you tell me what any of those are, specifically?"

"Hmm, well... If you knew specifically what you might find here, you *definitely* wouldn't have agreed to come with me."

"So, you lied to me again."

"Omitting the truth isn't *exactly* lying. Like I said, I will explain things as they become pertinent. If I just filled your head up willy-nilly with everything I know all at once, you'd never be able to keep it all straight. Your skull would explode. Besides, I took steps to protect you. I'm not a complete villain. Maybe you noticed that I applied a liberal helping of fresh garlic to your sandwich."

"Urgh, I definitely noticed more than a smidge of garlic, but I chalked that up to you bein' a bad—er, inexperienced chef."

"Well, that wasn't just for flavor. Garlic will protect you from most monsters that may want to do harm to you."

"Most, but not all?"

"The ones you'd at least stand a chance of running away from, anyway. For all the others, be glad you're at least carrying a shovel. And if that fails, you can rest assured that you will make a most delicious and well-seasoned entrée. Hoho!"

"Have you ever fought off a monster with nothing but a shovel?"

"I've never been foolish enough to try it. Rest assured though, if we cross paths with anything that wants to separate the parts of our bodies from one another, I'll be right there behind you."

Mortenson playfully tapped me on the shoulder with his cane, then continued walking, chuckling to himself as he went. With the gravity of the forest's perils thoroughly impressed on me, we marched on. Even though he had attempted to reassure me that the danger was manageable, I stuck close to the old man out of reverence and fear. It was no comfort at all that a bear might be one of the friendlier beasts we could encounter.

Chapter 26

With thoughts of Wendigos, witches and bears tormenting my mind, another disturbing realization came to me. If people bring their folkloric creatures with them when they move, did that mean that I may have brought one here from Tennessee? Had I unknowingly attracted a creature like the Not-Deer from its home to a new one where it could do all kinds of harm and destruction? It could be here right now, stalking us!

My mind began to race with my eyes, which darted back and forth across the secretive army of trees. Only darkness, in every direction. My lantern dimly illuminated the trees, toadstools, and the odd squirrel that chittered and scurried away when we drew near. Then, I saw it.

Deep in the distant trees and glittering through the blackness of tree-covered night, was a strange orange light. Fixated on this specter and fighting the urge to panic, I reached out to grab Mortenson to get his attention, and accidentally tugged on his beard.

"OORP!" he shouted as he spun around like a top. "Ouch! Why in heavens did you do that, boy?"

"Shhh!" I pointed toward the faint glow and said, "Mr. Mortenson, can you see that light?"

"Hmm, what's that? A light?" He took off his glasses and wiped them clean with his beard, placing them back on his nose. When this failed to reveal anything to him, he removed a spyglass from his coat pocket and pointed it in the general direction my finger indicated. "What do you know? You're right. There's something over there. Might be human, although I don't know who'd be foolish enough to be out here in the woods this late at night."

Self-Awareness was not something the old man practiced often, so his had totally atrophied.

"I don't think it *is* human, sir. I think it might be the Not-Deer."

"Not-Deer, hmm? You last saw it as a boy in Okabedokee, didn't you? What makes you think it might be that?"

"For the last time, sir, I grew up in Shroud's Creek. Okabedokee's in the Smokies. Anyway, I've been thinkin' about what you said, about how critters can stow away with humans when they move around."

"You think a Not-Deer followed you all the way from Tennessee to Pennsylvania? I suppose such a thing wouldn't be unheard of. You'd be surprised to learn what kind of creatures snuck aboard Columbus's ships. The conquistadors weren't the only monsters on board the Niña and Pinta."

The old man continued rambling while I watched the light. It appeared to be stationary, flickering ominously in the distance. If what we were seeing was the Not-Deer, then I was responsible for bringing it here, so I decided that we ought to act.

"We should go'n capture it," I proposed to my boss.

"Boy, have you taken leave of your senses? We aren't prepared to catch a Not-Deer. All we have are a pair of shovels, a lantern, a spyglass, and bellies full of garlic. Besides, we don't even know that's what it is."

"What if it is, though, and it starts a fire and burns down the forest? That would be on my hands."

"Remember that our purpose—our mission here—is to collect enough money to pay off the Landlord before midnight. If you don't abandon this nonsense and come along with me, *my* death may be on your hands," he grumbled, dramatically throwing the loose end of his beard over his shoulder and stomping off again deeper into the woods.

I trailed after him, insisting, "The woods might be in danger!"

"The woods are in no danger at all," the old man answered.

"How d'you know that?"

"It'll be just fine."

"That's no answer!"

"I'm assuming, okay? I don't have time for this, Gunnar. My life is on the line."

"Y'know, I just can't understand you, sir!" I yelled.

"What need have you to understand my ways? Do you have any idea about the responsibility I bear?"

"That's what I mean! You act like you have some kinda sacred duty to the folks o' Raspberry Hill, but all you really do is sell them snake oil. You say the heart and soul o' what y' do is stoppin' monsters, but when one crosses your path, you're more concerned about yourself!"

"I don't claim to be a hero, boy, and you'd be wise not to think of me as such."

"But ain'tcha got any sense of responsibility? Everythin' seems to come down to money with you."

"I wish I could just go about my life fulfilling every altruistic whim that comes into my head, but unfortunately it takes a lot of money to do what I do. Sometimes that means doing things that are unsavory or even morally questionable. Maybe someday things won't be like that, but until then, I'll go on selling my snake oil and just making sure that I prevent as much harm as I can."

"Respectfully speaking, sir, I can't accept that."

"You only think you can't because you're a young idealist. So was I, once. Just as I had to accept the way the world works, so will you eventually."

He turned his back to me and walked on, then. He clearly wanted this conversation to end, but I still had a fire in my brain that I hadn't quenched yet. I was still mad at Mortenson but couldn't think of an appropriate rebuttal at that point.

We walked on for some time in uncomfortable silence.

Perhaps it was his intention, but the silence gave me time to reflect, and I came to realize that although I felt as though he had hurt me, I had wounded him also. I thought that I ought to say something.

"Sir?" I called out with a crack in my voice.

"Yes, lad?" he answered coolly.

"I... I feel like I owe you an apology."

"What for?"

"You know what for. I lost my temper and got ornery with you."

"Oh, that. I'm no fool, I know how frustrating I can be to deal with. I'm surprised it took so long for you to come to a boil. Just know that I'm always trying to do the right thing, even though sometimes I have to make a cynical decision. Adult life is often about compromise, just as adolescent life is often about temperamental outbursts, heh!"

"I'll do my best to understand you better."

"And I, you. So then, all is forgiven."

"All's forgiven. I'm still concerned, though. Are you actually confident that the forest will be okay?"

"I know that it has survived worse. We're just two little humans in this gigantic world. The forest doesn't need us to protect it."

"I s'pose you're right. You know, you've got me good and worried about bein' here now, but you still didn't tell me any specific critters I ought to watch out for."

"Well, we're finally arrived at our destination, so you'll find out which creature we're concerned with soon. Take a look for yourself!"

There was suddenly a clearing in the woods which opened up to reveal the edge of a cliff, overlooking a small field that sat at the center of another cluster of trees at the base of a mountain. Never before in my life had I been able to gaze out and see for miles and miles around. I was, for the first time, above the rolling mountains, and the tops of the trees which seemed impossibly tall before.

It was a cloudless night, and the stars and moon provided celestial light for the view. At once, the terrifying mystery of the forest melted away and the atmosphere became picturesque and serene. My fear subsided, and I felt like the emperor of the universe on top of his mountain throne.

All was silent and still. The only sound was the wind dancing through the forest below. It was as though we were the only beings awake to witness this splendor and majesty.

Beautiful as it was, I assumed we weren't there to sightsee.

"So, we're here," I said. "What do we do now?"

"Sit down and get comfortable, son," Mortenson answered. "For now, we wait and see."

Chapter 27

So, there we were. In the middle of the night, lying belly down in the grass, with our noses hanging over the sheer cliff face that dropped down to the clearing below. Just myself, Mr. Mortenson, the moon, and the stars, which provided us with the only light we had to see by. We still had the lantern, and no, concerned reader, we had not run out of fuel, nor had the device suffered an operational malfunction.

No, none of these reasonable explanations were the cause as to why we had to lie there in the dark, possibly surrounded by creatures that wanted to turn us into ghosts. We were doing this because the old man instructed me to turn it off.

"Why?" I asked. "Ain't we waitin' for somethin' dangerous?"

"Potentially," he non-answered. "But if we keep ourselves hidden and be patient, we should be fine. Now, put out that light, lay down, and watch the tree line straight ahead. If you see movement, don't make a noise, but tap me on the shoulder."

"What am I lookin' for? You still haven't told me."

"You'll know it when you see it."

Despite how skeptical I was of him, Mortenson hadn't necessarily steered me wrong yet, so I complied and snuffed out the lantern. We both lowered ourselves to where the grass shrouded us and began to watch the forest. I employed the Hand-On-the-Eyebrows method of surveillance, and the old man scanned the tree line with his spyglass.

The tall grass was soft enough that laying on it was not uncomfortable, but I swiftly grew impatient. Seemingly endless time passed as Mr. Mortenson and I laid there, waiting. Minutes seemed to dilate and stretch on forever. Every time I looked back at my employer, he was unchanged, still gazing backward and forward along the plains below us, looking for who-knows-what.

It reminded me of that night when I was a boy, when I sat out on the porch of the family farm, trying to spot the mystery creature that was burning our crops. I had been lucky that night, both to encounter that elusive creature, and also to have made it out alive.

The memories of that night returned to me. The fear and anticipation of waiting and watching, the terror I felt when the Not-Deer and I met face-to-face, and the shame I felt when I was reprimanded by Pa. It all came back, then. Once again, I felt like the little boy who had gotten himself in way over his head.

I couldn't help then but wonder what Pa and Ma would think of this. They were probably at home, worried to tears about me. If they knew I was out in the woods hunting mysterious creatures with the eccentric old Curiosity dealer, I imagined that they would be disappointed or angry with me.

Doubt and guilt crept into my mind. Maybe this was a mistake, after all. I had no idea of the danger I might be in, and my companion was aloof at best.

An urgency to return home started to overtake me. I looked over to the old man again. He sat still as a statue frozen in time.

"Sir," I whispered. "Are you still awake?"

He didn't unglue the spyglass from his eye, but answered softly, "Of course I am, boy, and keep your voice down. We don't want to spook the creature that we're waiting for."

"What critter? We've been here for nearly an hour and

we ain't seen a thing."

"There'll be no mistaking when it finally emerges."

"What? Is it a... um... maybe a sasquatch?"

"Sasquatch? Pfffft!" he scoffed. "There's no such thing."

I said nothing at that, but just stared at him skeptically. He turned and took notice of the look I was giving him, and said, "What?"

I answered, "Squonks. Not-Deer. Wendigos. In the past few days, these are all things that you've confirmed are real. But sasquatch is out of the question?"

"Have you ever seen such a thing?"

"No, but others have said they have."

"Any fool can make any wild claim and dupe people into giving them attention and money for it. I will demonstrate that for you right now. Look up at the sky, lad. Can you point out the planet Jupiter?"

I twisted my neck to look up at the clear night sky. Of the millions of glowing dots that I could see, I failed to identify Jupiter among them.

"No, I can't find it."

"Okay, try this one. Can you point out the star called Gadriflax?"

I gave him one of my trademark incredulous stares for that question. "Now you're just yankin' my leg."

"Go on, show me where it is."

I sighed and answered, "There ain't no star Gadriflax. I reckon you made that up."

"How do you know that? You didn't even look. For that matter, how do you know Jupiter is real?"

"I know because there is evidence that Jupiter exists. Others have identified it, and if I knew where it was s'posed to be in the sky tonight, I could use a telescope to find it. There's no evidence—to my knowledge—of a star called Gadriflax existin'."

"Exactly! Likewise, there has never been convincing evidence that sasquatch is real. None that didn't turn out to be a hoax, anyway."

"Well then, we ought to look for evidence."

"That isn't how this works, boy. You can't just arrive at an answer and then look for evidence to support it. You have to follow the evidence to the conclusion. If you go to the doctor, do they give you a diagnosis before you describe one symptom to them? Not if the doctor is any good. No, a doctor makes their diagnosis based on observable facts."

I considered this and conceded that Mr. Mortenson was right.

It was then that I remembered the strange objects I had discovered in my great-aunt's secret room, and the bill of sale that showed Mortenson had sold them to her. These things were evidence that led to one conclusion: my boss's knowledge was the only missing piece to finish this puzzle.

While I had the old man in a conversational mood, I decided now would be a good opportunity to ask him about it.

"So, it would be foolish for me to claim that, say, fortune tellin' was real without anythin' to back it up," I proposed.

"That's right," Mortenson agreed.

"But if I had found, for example, an altar with candles, runic symbols, a crystal ball, and a receipt of sales from your records for all of these items, that would be pretty good evidence that it *is* real?"

Mortenson looked at me darkly and replied, "This isn't about research and discovery anymore, is it?"

"You sold fortune telling materials to my great-aunt Shannon. I found them in our house."

"Shannon Hollinger was your great-aunt?"

In the face of this obliviousness, it took all of my strength to resist the urge to bring my palm crashing into my forehead. "You didn't piece that together when you came to our house the other day?"

"I'm a tad reclusive if it had escaped your notice. I rarely leave my shop. I don't know whose house is whose. That was the first time I had ever stepped foot in there."

"And you didn't notice the massive portrait of her on our staircase?"

"I wasn't looking for paintings of great-aunts, I was looking for squonks. When I'm on the hunt, all else is invisible to me!"

"Never mind that, did you sell her a soothsaying set, or didn't you?"

"The records didn't lie; I did sell those things to her. You say you found the crystal ball in your house?"

"Yeah, in a secret room, on a small table surrounded by chalk runes and used candles. It was cracked in half."

"Ah, so she *did* use it, then..."

"Whatever she saw in it must have been awf'ly upsettin' for her to smash it like that."

"Hmm? Oh, no, no. You misunderstand. She couldn't have broken it herself. You see, a crystal ball is a one-time-use object. Peering into the future requires such a strong concentration of magic that the orb can't handle it for long and will shatter."

"Bein' able to see into the future seems like a pretty dangerous power. I'm surprised you would part with it when you don't even trust Ysabel with salted herring."

"I made an exception. It shouldn't be surprising to you, since Mrs. Hollinger was more trustworthy than any cat—most of all Ysabel—who one time faked illness so that I'd give her fresh fish for a full week."

"Why?"

"You've seen the lengths that cat will go to for a tasty snack."

"No, why did you make an exception for my great-aunt?"

"Ah, oh, yes. Raspberry Hill has a handful of wealthy families, and normally, I wouldn't trust any of those self-centered, high-society weasels with so much as a fortune cookie. A real scrying artifact would be, as you correctly assumed, totally out of the question. The Hollingers, particularly Shannon, were different from the others, however. They were well-liked in town, and contributed to the community, too.

"She was endlessly kind and generous, providing funding for the library and the fire department, to name just a of her charitable endeavors. She seemed to be close friends with everyone—save myself, perhaps, but only because I prefer to be an enigma—and everyone knew they could count on her for charity if they were desperate. Some might say she had *class*.

"So, her reputation preceded her when she came into my shop that one and only time many months ago.

"Instead of pretending to browse before approaching me, like most customers do, she came straight to me and directly asked if I knew of anything that would allow her to see into the future. I told her that, yes, I was aware that such a thing existed but that in the wrong hands it was too dangerous.

"I suppose I should have seen the family connection between you and her, because once I had given her that little crumb, she was determined to sniff out the whole loaf, as it were. She kept pressing and asking questions. Finally, she got me to admit that what she was after was a crystal ball, and indeed, I was in possession of one. With that, I explained to her that she could ask it any question regarding the future, and it would show her the answer.

"She insisted that she would buy it from me and asked me to name my price. I was adamant, though, that such a thing was not to be trifled with by just anyone. Knowing one's own future, I explained, is a dangerous thing that can lead one to make catastrophic choices.

"She told me then that she already knew her *own* future. Her doctor had recently diagnosed her with a terminal illness and gave her at most another month to live. She said that if she had a crystal ball, the question she would ask it was, 'How can I make sure my nephew's family are taken care of?' They hadn't spoken in so long that they lost contact and she wanted to give her beloved nephew one more gift before she died.

"I could tell that she was sincere, and despite how

shrewd I am, I'm not heartless. I relented and sold her the crystal ball, the rune guide, and the candles for a reasonable price. After that, I never saw her again, and true enough, news of her passing swept through town a few weeks later."

I was beside myself, shocked and delighted.

It explained everything. How she was able to answer my father's letter. How she supplied the house for us, furniture, clothes, and all. She must have used the crystal ball and saw what my father would write to her so that she could write a response, prepare her will, and orchestrate our coming to Raspberry Hill before she died.

The revelation of my great-aunt's final act of charity to my family nearly brought tears to my eyes. However, my revelry was interrupted. There suddenly rose a terrible noise, like roaring thunder, from the tree line below us.

 # Chapter 28

"A-ha!" Mortenson gasped. Using the crook of his cane, he pressed down on my head so I would lay back down in the grass. He stuck the spyglass in my eye, muttering, "Look out there, lad, and keep quiet! The creature awakes!"

I looked through the small telescope and watched as a cluster of trees started stretching and twisting at the trunk. The branches and leaves rustled violently as, to my surprise, four of the tree trunks began to bend as if they had elbows and knees.

The two trees in front leaned over, and then hoisted themselves out of the ground. As the roots flew skyward, there emerged from each hole in the ground a pair of colossal, greyish-green hands. The fingernails were black from the soil crammed under them, and bits of debris and moss crumbled to the Earth as the hands arose, poked their fingers into the branches, and scratched the body that was concealed within.

Behind these humongous arms, another pair of tree trunks lifted out of the soil, one after the other, to reveal that connected to them were a pair of schooner-sized feet. One came up out of the dirt and slammed down on the grass with a thundering THUD, then the other, in a duo of earth-shaking stomps.

The nature of this bizarre transformation was now clear to me. What had appeared previously to be a cluster of trees was actually a gigantic body in camouflage. It was a humanoid biped, dressed in a cloak of tree branches and leaves that shrouded its head and chubby torso, with tree bark wrapped around its limbs.

The giant raised a hand up to the darkened area where its mouth was barely visible in the moonlight. It opened its cavernous jaw, revealing a set of gnarly, blocky, brownish-yellow teeth and a tongue that flapped and dripped like a pink flag in a hurricane. A slow, laborious breath was drawn in, then it yawned, the gale force of which blew my hair back and brought tears to my eyes. Its breath smelled like freshly plowed earth after a heavy rain.

It scratched its belly though its shirt of foliage, then started to take lumbering steps forward, each one crashing down with a force that made craters underfoot. Its knuckles dragged on the ground, plowing up rocks and uprooting grass. It was at this moment that I realized something important.

"Um, Mr. Mortenson," I muttered, leaning in close so that I could be heard over the booming footsteps.

"Breathtaking, isn't it?" the old man mused.

"By thunder, it truly is. There's just one thing. Now, I don't want to alarm you, but that giant is headin' toward us."

"Of course, it is. It's coming to feed," the old man answered helpfully.

"Okay, now *I'm* alarmed."

"Don't worry, lad. What you see before you is a mountain troll. Fret not, we're not on the menu, because this creature is a strict geovore."

"You mean it eats rocks?"

"That's right. Usually it lives in mountain caves, feeding on the stones from its personal quarry. But every now and again, when it has the craving for a delicacy like cliffside stone, it will venture outside to collect it."

"And we don't have anythin' to fear from it?"

"Not so long as we're up here where it can't accidentally step on us. These trolls prefer to stay far away from humans if they can help it."

"So, like how elephants are scared of mice?"

"Hmm? No, that doesn't make sense. Why would any creature be afraid of another creature it could flatten with one footstep? You aren't afraid of spiders, are you?"

"I'm not personally, but there're many people who are."

"Is that true? Maybe the trolls see us as creepy crawlies, then. Who knows? But look now and see what it does."

The troll came to a halt before us but had not noticed our presence. It raised one titanic paw and gripped a piece of the cliff, breaking off a sizable slab. It brought the stone to its face and sniffed deeply, the force of which nearly yanked me over the edge. Its mammoth tongue extended and gave the crust a taste test.

The behemoth licked its lips and then smacked them together with a noise like tidal waves crashing against a pier. The troll grumbled with dissatisfaction and looked around for something to enhance the flavor.

It leaned over, dragging the slab through a patch of mud. Next, it plucked a streak of chalk from the cliff face, grinding it up between its gargantuan fingers and sprinkling it on top for seasoning. Lastly, a scraping of moss was applied to serve as a garnish.

With the recipe completed, the troll opened its mouth wide and chomped down hard on the meal it had crafted. A piece broke off between its teeth with a bone-shattering CRACK! It chewed happily and so noisily that I had to cover my ears to protect them from the deafening grinding of stone.

Several more pieces of mud-covered, artisanally-seasoned slab were produced and consumed until the giant was satisfied, grumbling to itself with delight. It stuck its pinky nail between its teeth, extracted a twig, and flicked it away.

Then, to my horror, there arose from the belly of the beast a rumbling, thunderous noise, which gained power and momentum up through its chest, finally manifesting in a single explosive belch. The force of this gassy maelstrom stripped the trees behind us of their leaves and caused several branches to come crashing to the ground.

Finally, the troll turned away from us, paused, and then crouched beside the cliff. With a powerful, bellowing grunt, a landslide poured out underneath it, creating a massive heap of gravel and soil on the ground. It stood back up and scratched its backside before sauntering off, returning to the dark depths of the forest.

"Marvelous!" beamed Mr. Mortenson. "Have you ever seen anything to match that?"

"No, not quite to that scale, I reckon. Although a cow can come close," I replied truthfully. "So, now what?"

"Isn't it obvious, lad?" he answered, raising his shovel aloft and waving it about.

A horrifying realization dawned on me as everything finally added together. "Oh, noooooooo..." I groaned.

"That's right. Grab your shovel, son. We're going digging."

Chapter 29

THERE HAPPENED TO BE—unfortunately—a narrow and steep pathway that allowed us to climb down to the bottom of the cliff, where the troll had—unfortunately—done its business. This meant that there were no excuses—unfortunately—and there was no way for me to get out of dealing with what my boss had in mind for it.

Unfortunately.

"Fortunate that there happens to be a way down here!" the old man said gleefully.

He was surprisingly nimble, using the shovel like a second cane and hopping from stone to stone on the descent toward the bottom. Perhaps it was anticipation that put the leap in his step, and reluctance that sapped it from mine.

We reached the foot of the cliff, and I stood before the enormous heap of digested earth. Disturbingly, it was still warm, and wisps of steam rose off of it in the chilly night air. The stench put me in mind of fresh fertilizer, but at a severally multiplied intensity. Not all the aromatic candles in the world could mask this outrageous smell. In fact, nothing short of severing the nose from the face would.

My stomach wretched and I nearly doubled over in disgust. My belly was doing flips and spins, and so was the old man as he paced excitedly around it.

"Magnificent! Exemplary! Astounding!" he was muttering.

"Please tell me that this ain't what I think it is," I

groaned.

"No ifs, ands, or buts about this, well, apart from maybe one. Hoho! I told you that a mountain troll lives most of its life in its cavern home, feasting on the stone below the surface. If I'm correct, that should mean we have a nice pile of fully digested rock from deep underground."

Mortenson lifted his shovel and drove it into the steamy, earthy mound, and extracted a handful of loam. It made a crunchy, squelching sound as he did so.

"Just as I thought!" he announced. "The droppings left by this mountain troll are entirely and totally metamorphic! Wholly schist!"

"Beggin' your pardon?"

"It means that in this hefty pile there's a good chance that we'll find..." he sifted his fingers through the small pile of damp soil, and produced a small, glittering stone. "Gold! The body can't break it down, so it simply passes through the digestive system out the other end."

"Stop, stop, stop," I protested. "We are *not* about to go diggin' through a troll's leavin's to look for gold. That's disgustin'."

"What? It's only soil and gravel. It's sanitary. Don't be so squeamish. If this is too much for you, you'd faint to hear how sausages and cheese are made. Would you still eat honey if you knew how bees made it?"

I gazed regretfully on the mound again and whined, "Do I have to?"

"This is the job, lad. Sometimes it means getting your hands dirty. Of course, I wouldn't blame you if you wanted to resign. Not many are cut out for the sort of work I do."

I couldn't let that backhanded comment go unanswered, so I rolled up my sleeves, gritted my teeth, and dug my shovel into the grit. The old man chuckled and the two of us set about our task.

For the next half hour, we shifted schist and sifted... well, you know. The first shovelful was the worst. I just had to force myself to think of it as soil and soil only. In that mindset, it was no different from working on the family farm. I had mucked out the chicken coop many times before. Comparatively, the odor and the texture of this pile were more bearable.

After a while, I got used to my hands being covered in filth, and I stopped noticing when a plump, wriggly worm stuck to my wrist. I would simply raise a lump of earth, probe my fingers about, and extract any solid nuggets I discovered. I started to miss the accounting work from earlier this afternoon.

In fairness, every time I work on accounting now, I long for the shovel, either to dig through sludge or to bury myself with.

Most of the hard bits were rocks and gravel, but every so often a shimmering piece of gold would turn up, and I would pocket it. Once, I was shocked to find a tiny diamond, no bigger than the tip of a pencil, and I showed it to my employer. He laughed and said that it was good luck, and it meant I could make a wish.

I wished for a hot bath.

Once we had carefully picked through every grain of the heap and separated it into two piles (mine suspiciously larger than his), we examined the fruits of our labor. A hefty collection of gold nuggets, which barely fit into both of Mortenson's cupped palms, was poured into a burlap sack and tied up.

The old man congratulated me on a job well done, giving me a friendly slap on the back, which left a muddy handprint on my nice white shirt. These clothes were definitely getting thrown out, and possibly burned when I finally got home.

"Excellent work, lad!" he beamed. "This looks like it will be enough to pay off the Landlord!"

I replied, "I hope so. He should at least appreciate what went into gettin' it."

"Hmm, I'm afraid the Landlord is a literalist when it comes to value. All that matters is the object and its material worth. I found that out the hard way when, one year, I managed to obtain the King of Atlantis's scepter, which was no easy task, as you can imagine."

"No, sir, I don't think I can."

"I'll have to tell you the tale someday. Anyway, I had hoped that the trouble I went to for it paired with its significance would make it utterly priceless. The Landlord disagreed. Luckily, its value in gold and jewels was enough to cover the d—the RENT for that year."

"Oh. What was that you were about to say?"

"Nothing, nothing. Midnight approaches, and we have but an hour to get back to the shop! I have a chest of valuables that we'll add this too, and when the Landlord arrives, we will hand it all over."

Chapter 30

And so, we retraced our steps back up the slope, and through the forest. I was allowed to turn the lantern back on, but we were in such high spirits at that point that it mattered little. We could have run into the Devil himself and our confidence wouldn't have been tarnished in the least.

What spoiled things was when I noticed Mortenson pausing at intervals with concerned eyebrows, before continuing on, seeming confused and disoriented. At several points, he stopped and remarked on the familiarness of a tree or boulder. I started to grow terrified as I realized that my boss was hopelessly lost.

"Sir," I murmured, "you *do* know the way back to Raspberry Hill, don't you?"

"Of course, I do, Gunnar. I've been through these woods countless times, I know them intimately well," he answered while experimentally tapping a tree trunk with his cane.

"Are we lost?"

"I'm never lost! Just a little... bewildered at the moment... Blast! Which way is North?"

He turned his gaze to the sky above, but instead of the tableau of constellations and nebulae which had hung over us previously, clouds now covered it entirely. The north star, and in fact the entire night sky was totally obscured.

"Odd..." he mused. "Sudden overcast, that isn't good."

"Didn't you bring a compass?" I asked.

"Right! I did remember to bring one of those," he said, turning out his pockets until he found the navigation tool. My relief was short-lived, however, as when we took a look at the compass, we found the needle spinning wildly, as if it were eager to break out and fly away.

"This is a normal compass, right?" I inquired. "You didn't, by mistake, bring a magical compass that points toward forest goblins?"

"No, it's a normal compass; the goblin compass wouldn't do us any good in *these* woods, where there are none. But maybe there's something wrong with the Earth's magnetic field, or this one has lost calibration." He looked around and brightened up when he spotted something. "Ah-ha! But we may not be sunk yet!"

Mortenson shambled over to an old, vine-covered tree, at the base of which was a patch of little, white toadstools. He knelt down and surveyed the bed of fungus.

"We're in luck, my boy! This is a grove of chat-talky mushrooms," he happily announced.

"With all due respect, I believe that's said *shiitake*, sir. Shee-Tocky."

"Hush, boy, I know what a shiitake mushroom is."

"I don't see how mushrooms help us get out of this forest. Can we cook 'em to make some kinda navigatin' potion?"

"We're not going to eat them. Heavens, no! Just quiet down and watch, boy. Hello, hello, hello!" he called out over the small white mounds.

At first, there was no response, but slowly, there was movement in the grove. One by one, each of the ivory caps tilted up to reveal a face on the stalk, each one the visage of a wrinkly, chubby old man. They gazed around at one another with puzzled expressions and blinked their sleepy eyes.

The largest cap, clearly the mushroom monarch, yawned, regally cleared its throat, and then spoke.

"Errr... huh?" it said. This was followed by a chorus of

what?'s, wuzzit?'s, and *hmm?'s* from the rest of the cluster. All I could do was throw up my hands in defeat. "I just need to stop bein' surprised by things," I said to my boss. "These little fellas can tell us the way out of the forest?"

Mortenson stood to explain, "All of the plants and fungus in a forest are connected by a complicated network of roots, by which they can communicate. A tree on one end of the woods will know if there is a drought on the opposite side. Such a complex web of communication as this may never be replicated by human technology! The chat-talkies should know which way we have to go in order to return to Raspberry Hill." He knelt down again and addressed the toadstools. "Hello, my little friends! Good evening!"

Several of them looked drowsily at him, blinking their unfocused eyes at him and mumbling, "Hmm? Wuzzit?" and "Errr... huh?"

"If it's not too much trouble, could any of you tell me the way to get to the town of Raspberry Hill?"

"Raspberry Hill? Errr... I think it's that way," answered one, pointing its nose in one direction.

"No, don't be daft," disagreed another. "You're thinking of Blackberry Hill, where the brown bears and gnomes live. The one these humans want is in the other direction."

"Errr... huh?" contributed another.

"No, no, *Raspberry* Hill," the old man insisted. "The human settlement. Surely you know which direction we have to go to find it?"

One plump sprout with squinty old eyes stretched itself as tall as it could muster and insisted, "As sure as my cap is white, it's that way."

"No, by my spores! You're all wrong! It's THAT way."

"Errr... huh?"

Mortenson was feeling embarrassed and frustrated, and tried asking a different question. "Okay, okay, never mind Raspberry Hill. Can you at least tell us which way is north?"

The entire patch of chat-talkies was now engaged in a

heated debate. Everyone was pointing in a different direction and shouting. One pitifully confounded mushroom was staring straight down at the ground, insisting that maybe north had gone down there. It was beginning to get personal.

"Listen to me, you lumps! North is that way."

"You old fool. You don't know the difference between yeast and mold, let alone north and south."

"You can always tell which way north is by the side of a tree the bark grows on. Or is it the branches? Or the... ummmm..."

"Don't listen to him. All you have to do is put a stick in the ground and see which direction the shadow points."

"What shadow? It's the middle of the night!"

"They have a... wuzzit? A lantern. Errr... is that helpful?"

"Bless Your... well, not your heart," I sarcastically replied. "Whatever it is that you have instead."

Mortenson stood back from the confused cluster, dumbfounded to find them so dumb.

"I don't understand," he cried out over the confusion. "Any plant or fungus in the woods ought to be able to tell where anything else is. A fly can't land on a lily pad without a daffodil five miles away feeling a mysterious tickle." He pondered for a minute, and then said, "I have a theory, lad, that I want to test. Stand here."

The old man placed me in a seemingly random spot in the grass. I then watched him search around until he found a rock, palm-sized and distinctly heart-shaped. He stood next to me and showed me the stone.

"See this, here?" he asked. "Watch me, now."

He proceeded to hurl the rock straight ahead. It vanished in the darkness, and moments later, something came flying from behind and clonked me in the back of the skull.

"OW! What in tarnation!?" I yelled, spinning around to see what had hit me. Mr. Mortenson leaned down and picked up... the heart-shaped rock. The very same one he had flung away from us in the opposite direction.

"Ooh, this is bad," he uttered.

"You're darn right!" I raged. "That smarts!"

"Listen to me, Gunnar. I'm positive that someone is trying to prevent us from leaving the forest. We're trapped in some kind of bewilderment spell. That would explain the compass needle, the rock, and the chat-talkies' confusion. Illusions, the warping of space and direction, and the sudden shift in the weather, all part of an elaborate ruse to keep us here in the Devils' Forest."

Chapter 31

THE REVELATION THAT WE might be trapped by a malicious magician in the malignant forest was the most disquieting of all that night. My mind immediately turned to action.

"How do we break the spell?" I asked.

Mr. Mortenson stroked his beard ponderously and replied, "The only way out is through. We need to find the spellcaster, and right quick, too. If the clock hits midnight, the Landlord will come and that'll be the end of me."

"He can find us anywhere we're at? He ain't human, is he?"

"No, not as such."

"What if this is bein' done *by* the Landlord to sabotage us?"

"That's not how the Landlord operates. While fearsome and unstoppable, he's fair. He won't do anything to hinder or help us, he'll just show up at midnight—no matter where we are—to collect. If we don't have the money with us, he'll take my life instead."

"What if it's some kinda critter that wants to kill us, or worse?"

"I don't know of any creatures that can perform this kind of magic. This has to be the work of a human spellcaster."

"And I imagine they won't just stop if we say 'please,' huh?"

"Nothing worth doing is ever easy, son. Odds are, if we

keep moving, we'll be led to the one who put the spell on the forest. I can't think of anyone who would want to kill us... well, *you*, at any rate, so they must want something else, and will lead us right to them."

"And if they do want to kill us?"

"Then we'll have to find some way to prevent them from doing it. Let's move along, now."

It was no consolation to me that our yet-unseen assailant was human. As we moved through the woods, the continuing argument and occasional muttering of "errr... huh?" of the chat-talky mushrooms faded into nothingness and once again, there was nothing but the ambiance of nature.

Eventually, I could hear a faint noise, a high pitch chattering that rose with every step. As we pressed on, it grew to a noisome screeching, and looking up, I could see there was a congregation of squirrels, hopping along with us from branch to branch, looking down and chirping at us.

"Hmm, some guidance, finally. Graciously considerate of them," Mortenson observed. If he hadn't said that I may have panicked, because *my* interpretation was that they were getting ready to swarm and attack.

Further and further on, led by the squirrels overhead, the fog started to clear, and the trees parted to form a path. Through the blackness of night, a faint glow pierced my vision. Ahead of us was an orange light, which I recognized as the same one I had noticed before. This time, however, it was possible to distinguish its source.

The light was coming from the window of a cottage that was built into a large, grassy mound beneath a massive old oak tree. Scattered all around it were a multitude of multicolored toadstools and dead leaves. These, however, had nothing useful, or even useless to say to us. It was still late August, but this mysterious abode definitely had an October atmosphere to it.

The windows and doors of the hut were placed between the tree's roots. At the front was a set of cobblestone steps leading down to a wooden door with runes written on it with blue paint. Hanging from the branches above were a variety of charms and amulets, all with a motif of stars, moons, planets, and the occasional asteroid. A knothole in the trunk was belching smoke like a chimney.

The squirrels of the forest excitedly ran up and down this tree, entering through the open windows. Some of them were carrying flowers, roots, and other ingredients. Within, the sound of a woman's voice could be heard giving them indistinguishable commands. A few of them hopped around our legs, beckoning us to approach the door.

"Mr. Mortenson," I said apprehensively, "this looks an awful lot like a witch's hut."

He replied, "Keep your voice down, lad. I can confirm that it has all the tell-tale qualities of a witch's hut, and as such, we have to practice tact."

"You said there weren't any witches in the forest!"

"No, I said that I didn't know of any. I wasn't even lying by omission this time. This cottage was heretofore totally unknown to me."

"What do we do?"

"We'll go inside, have a chat, see if I can get her to release us from the spell. Follow my lead, and don't say anything that might offend her."

"What sort of things offend a witch?"

Mortenson bobbed his head side to side indecisively and answered, "It differs from one witch to another. Some hate it when you point out their warts, some hate it when you pretend to ignore them. Others don't like mentions of fire. And never, ever, EVER speculate about her buoyancy. As it happens, this is also excellent advice for conversing with people in general, witch or not."

Mortenson descended the stairs and unwound his beard, licked his palms, and slicked the length of it to optimize its attractiveness and remove errant blades of grass and leaves. He extended a fist to knock on the door. Before he could though, and in accordance with narrative con-

Josh Berliner

vention, the door opened on its own, with a CREEEEAAAAK for good measure. The old man jumped back in surprise, and from within the warm, orange glow of the cottage, came a voice.

"EEE-HEE-HEE!" it cackled. "Come on in, dearies. Come on in!"

Chapter 32

Apprehensively, Mortenson followed the mysterious voice's command to enter, and I stuck closely behind him. Now, if you ever find yourself in the position where you and your employer have to enter the creepy cottage of an unknown assailant who is using magic to lure you in—and it *could* happen—I do not recommend, by any means, that you should follow them.

What you should do instead is anything else. Run in the opposite direction. Disguise yourself as a woodland beast. Anything is better than stepping foot into a witch's hut.

At the time, however, I didn't know enough to consider my options, so the pair of us went inside. The old man had entered in front of me, so at least I had *that* in case things should go pear-shaped. I just had to trust that he knew enough to handle the situation or was structurally sound enough to absorb any spells that might be cast at us.

The inside of the hut was warm and abuzz with activity, owing to the squirrels bustling about. Like Mortenson's storeroom, it was much larger on the inside. It had the same surreal orange light, but this was augmented by dozens of candles placed randomly about, which burned with violet, green, blue, and even black flames.

The perimeter of the room held all of the furniture and amenities that one would want for their home, but in a scattershot arrangement that begged for the professional help of an interior decorator. Tables were stacked on other tables, and held a variety of raw ingredients, candles, scrolls, and other suspicious objects which I had no interest in familiarizing myself with. A potbelly stove sat between two tables, which was heating up a tea kettle, and all of the other greasy pots and pans that were stacked on it.

A bed was balanced on the ends of two different tables and hung over the washbasin where dirty clothes floated in soapy water. Two of the bed's legs were shorter than the others, so it tilted toward the center of the room. A second dingy mattress was laid on the floor below as a safety precaution. On top it held a mountain of quilts with occult-seeming designs on them, and exactly one pillow which had been worn down so far that it resembled the humps of a camel.

Where there could have been wall space were shelves, which were overstuffed with yet more candles, scrolls, dishes, cups, and the odd vegetable or two. The floor of the cottage would have been nothing but dirt if not for a patchwork of rug fragments, which had been assembled from a collection of presumably discarded floor coverings and sewn together with twine.

At the center of the hut was a cast iron cauldron, bubbling over a fireplace and bellowing steam up to a chimney that hung directly over it. I hoped and prayed that I wouldn't have to find out what the sickly green liquid sloshing around in it was. On the other side of the cauldron from us was a tall, pointy hat that swayed back and forth. A voice, high-pitched and wheezy, came from it.

"By the cracking of my toes, something wycked thys way goes!" it said with a peculiar accent.

Mortenson thought carefully and then replied, "Nothing wicked, madame, I assure you. Just a pair of lost travelers."

"I wasn't talking about you, deary. Such a handsome duo you are. EEE-HEE! Here, you, take thys ladle and keep styrring." The order was directed to a gray squirrel who was perched on the lip of the cauldron. It took the soup ladle from the hidden figure, dipped it into the greenish concoction, and started to run laps around the circumference.

"My, you certainly seem to have a lot of help here," Mortenson said, acknowledging the multitude of squirrels which scurried about the cottage.

"Squirrels really are a gyrl's best friend out here," the hat answered. "I used to have a black cat, but it was so lazy and unrelyable. Squirrels are *far* easyer to control."

The entire place was busy as a beehive, with squirrels performing all sorts of chores. Some of them were bringing in ingredients from the forest and finding shelves or table space to store them. Others were hard at work chopping vegetables, which were handed off to yet more who climbed across the roof to drop them into the pot.

One solitary squirrel was hard at work scrubbing the laundry in the washbasin. On its shoulder there perched a cricket, which hopped up and down excitedly when I noticed it. There was something strangely familiar about that rodent, but at that moment, I couldn't quite place what it was.

There had to be powerful magic at work here. I felt the familiar sparkling sensation of enchanted air in my lungs as I breathed the pungent atmosphere. It all smelled like... like...

"Asparagus and cabbage stew?" offered the figure who jumped out from behind her bubbling cauldron while I was looking around. I tried to keep my eyes inside my head as I finally got a full view of our captor.

She was a short and spherical old lady, with long, unkempt, pink hair that draped over both of her shoulders. Her pointy, wide brimmed hat was about twice as tall as she was. This gave her the overall shape of an ice cream cone held upside-down.

Her face, a spiderweb of wrinkles, displayed a proud, toothy grin, or at least as toothy as a grin can be when some of the teeth are missing and those remaining can't agree which direction they should be pointing. She had milky eyes that couldn't help but broadcast the gleeful mischief they were trying to conceal. Contrary to the stereotype, she did not have a long, hooked nose with warts, but a small, button one.

Even standing perfectly still, the dozens of charm necklaces and bracelets she wore jingled and jangled as they brushed against her purple hemp dress. Dangling from her ears were a pair of earrings made from acorns. The sound of all this jewelry had blended into the general clatter of the squirrels going about their work, but in any other setting, the noise generated by her decorations would make her noticeable from miles away.

This was a woman dressed to impress every conceivable sensation—Impress, here meaning to push down on something and leave a mark, as she could flatten sight, touch, taste, hearing, and especially smell.

"Thank you, kindly, for that offer." Mortenson replied, referring to the bubbling brew that filled the cottage with its odor. "We've already eaten, so there's no need for us to trouble you further than we already have."

"Oh, nonsense! I'm just a lonely old woman who never gets vysitors. It would break my heart if you wouldn't accept a lyttle of my hospytality. Won't you at least take some tea?"

"Tea would be most... gracious of you."

"Splendyd! You two there!" she barked at a pair of idle squirrels, who snapped to attention. "Pour us some cups, with mylk and sugar. You take mylk and sugar, don't you?"

"Er, no sugar for me tonight, thank you."

"No sugar for the gentlemen, and as much as you can fyt in myne!" With that, the squirrels got to work.

Mortenson cleared his throat and asked, "And to whom do we owe our thanks?"

The old woman twirled around and with a flourish of the wrist said, "I'm known as Mystress Ethel Myndelom, but you can call me 'Mindy'. What do I have the pleasure of calling you?"

"Levi Mortenson, good lady, and this is—"

Here she interrupted him. "I assume the boy isn't mute, is he? You can speak, can't you, boy?"

Nervously, I answered, "Name's Gunnar, ma'am. Gunnar Shuck."

"Ooooh, that's a very handsome accent you have there. A southerner if I'm not mystaken?"

"Yes, ma'am, and, um, you've also got a nice accent... ma'am."

"I'm not sure whych accent you are indycating, but thank you."

Mortenson shoved me behind him and said, "Never mind him, he's just nervous and tired because, you see, we appear to have lost our way in the woods."

"Heavens!" Mindy gasped theatrically. "You don't say!"

"Yes, and we are in a terrible rush to get back to Raspberry Hill, so we shan't impose on you for long."

As Mortenson was saying this, the tea-serving squirrels brought the old man and I a teacup on a saucer each, balanced on their bushy tails, and filled with steaming hot fluid.

As we picked up our drinks, the old man said, "Okay, just one cup of tea, and then we'll be off." He raised the cup to his lips and made a face of enjoyment. "My, this is marvelous tea! Gunnar, don't you agree?" He elbowed me and I took a sip myself.

True enough, it was actually delicious tea. Not quite as good as Ma's sweet tea, but my expectations for a beverage brewed in a dingy cottage in the forest were exceeded.

"This is mighty fine tea, ma'am," was my review.

"It certainly is!" Mortenson injected before I could continue. "Do I detect a hint of hazelnut?"

"It's my own special recype! I'm glad you enjoy it."

"Yes, yes. We'll finish our cups and then if you wouldn't mind giving us directions to get back to Raspberry Hill?"

"Oh, why do you want to go to such a boring place as that? Surely, I'm far more intryguing and entycing to you?" she cooed, placing a bony hand under her fuzzy chin.

"I'm sure you're an excellent host, and I'll be sure to keep it in mind for the future, but it really is most urgent that we get back."

"Why? So you can put away that lyttle bag of gold you took from *my* woods?"

Mortenson's face darkened. "How do you know...?"

"The squirrels are my eyes and ears in the forest," she explained ominously. "I've been aware of you trespassing in my woods for years, and yet you never pay me a vysit. So, when they told me you had brought a young man with you thys tyme, I knew I just *had* to have you over. I'm just a poor, lyttle old lady with popping knees and an achy spyne. I can always use more help around the house from an able-bodied young gentleman."

"But... it looks like you have plenty of squirrels to do your chores for you," I said diplomatically.

"Oh, but I could always use at *least* one more," Mindy answered, her grin creeping into devilish territory.

With that sinister utterance, I became aware of a peculiar sensation in my gut. It started as a tingling that spread out to my limbs, and eventually across my whole body. Suddenly, the room and everything in it seemed to be expanding. I could feel my clothes getting baggy, until they laid on top of me like bed sheets.

Poking my face out from my clothes, I stared up at the horrified face of Mr. Mortenson and the delighted one of Ethel Myndelom, who both now towered over me. I looked down at my arms and saw that they were covered in bright orange fur and the hands at each end had been replaced by paws. Lastly, a big, bushy tail sprouted from my back side, and my transformation was complete.

"*SQUEAK!*" I squeaked.

"EEE-HEE-HEE-HEE-HEEEEEEE!" cackled the old witch.

"Gunnar! Did you actually drink the tea? I thought you knew I was faking it!" Mortenson scolded.

"*Squee-squeak!*" I protested, stomping my paw furiously.

Cryptid Currency

This simply made Mindy hop about with wicked glee. "EEE-HEE-HEE! Look at you now, lyttle red squirrel-boy! What kynd of chore would you lyke to do for me? You could organize my candle collection. There are lots of dyrty socks that need to be washed. Or maybe you could use that fluffy tayl to dust out the cobwebs?"

"You change my shop assistant back to a human this instant and release us from your enchantments!" Mortenson demanded.

"My, my, my, what happened to that gentlemanly demeanor you had only moments ago? Don't tell me you were faking that, too? It's not nyce to try to tryck innocent old ladies."

"Don't try that with me! You've been using your magic to lure men from the town here, change them into squirrels and make them do your bidding, haven't you?"

"*Chip-chip squeak!*" I chimed in.

"So what? They never come of their own accord. It's the least they could do synce they have a wytch as splendyd as myself near their otherwyse boring lyttle town. Besydes, I always send them back when I'm fynyshed with them. They wake up in their beds believing they've merely just had the *strangest* dream."

Mortenson bargained, "I'll give you all the gold I'm carrying if you change him back."

"*Squah-squeak?*" I asked.

"What use have I for sylly gold? I thynk it's ugly, and anyway, people have a habyt of gyving me thyngs that I would be more than happy to pay for."

"What is it you want from us, then?"

"Nothing more than a byt of entertainment, lovie! It gets so dull out here by my lonesome."

"Well then, if we're playing games, how about I propose another one?"

"Go on."

"Are you familiar with the rules of The Ochre King's Court?"

"Of course! I was the champyon player in my last

coven, and I always keep a deck of cards handy."

"Very well, then. I'd like to make a wager with you. If I can beat you, you have to turn Gunnar back into a human and lift all of the enchantments you've placed over the woods so we can go home."

The witch rubbed her hands together slyly and answered, "It's a deal. EEE-HEE-HEE! Squirrels! Fetch a table, two chairs, and my playing deck!"

Suddenly, I felt compelled to act, and my body began to move without my permission. I joined the squirrels of the hut, and we worked in unison to extract an empty table and two chairs from the cluster of furniture against the wall and set them next to the bubbling cauldron. Another squirrel climbed up on the table carrying in its teeth a stack of ancient, wrinkled cards that were bundled together with twine and set it down in the center.

Mindy swiped the deck in her hands and unbound them. "We'll play best two out of three," she said as she started shuffling the cards.

"Can't we just play best one out of one?" Mortenson asked sheepishly. "Only, I really am in a dreadful hurry and it's a matter of life or death."

"I could always just turn you into a squirrel as well. I'm being more than fayr," she insisted.

"Very well, then. Deal the cards and we'll play."

Chapter 33

Myndelom the witch laid down five cards each for Mortenson and herself, and the opponents looked at the hands they'd been dealt. Mortenson's face remained unchanged, but Mindy grinned cunningly.

"You go fyrst," she said. "Age before beauty, you know."

"I'm aware of the rules," grumbled the old man.

Now, I had never heard of The Ochre King's Court before, and as I climbed up onto the table to watch the action of the game, I just had to trust that my boss knew what he was doing. What followed was totally incomprehensible to me, and as much as I've tried to study this game afterward, I still don't understand it.

But this is how it played out.

Mortenson gently laid down a card with a picture of a jester juggling a variety of tools.

"I'll begin by playing the Jack of All Trades," he announced.

"Ooh, a strong opening move."

"Indeed, it allows me to draw two cards this turn," and he did so.

"I'll open with an aggressyve play of my own, the Ace of Space!" She slapped down the card and it showed a lone man gasping for breath as he floated among the stars. "That means I can take a card from your hand." She extended her bony fingers and extracted a card from Mortenson's collection. "EEE-HEE-HEE! Oops, you'll be myssing that card."

"That does put me in a bit of a bind, but luckily, I have the Salubrious Knave. Discard your hand and draw five more cards."

"Rats!" she exclaimed, and several squirrels recoiled in fear when she did. "Not you!"

She discarded her hand near the draw pile and took five new cards from it. Next, she considered her options and set down another card beside the Ace. "I'll counter with the Compulsyve Slug! Pyck one of your own cards to play on my behalf."

"If you insist. Have the Queen of Green Beans."

"Curses! I was hoping you dydn't have that card!"

"Yes, madam, and as you know, paired with the Ace of Space means an instant loss. This round goes to me."

"*Squeaky squeak!*" I exclaimed in triumph.

"Don't celebrate too early, boy! There are styll two more rounds. Your turn to deal, Levi."

Mortenson collected the cards and shuffled them. His arthritic hands were unexpectedly dexterous, making the cards seem to float in the air as they enmeshed with one another.

Mindy impatiently shouted, "Enough theatrycs! Deal the cards."

Mortenson did so, and this round, the witch had the opening move.

"I'll start with the Kyng of Potatoes, whose eyes allow me to see every card in your hand!"

"Oh, bother," Mortenson grumbled, and complied. Mindy took a good look at his hand and smiled.

"Well, well, it was awfully consyderate of you to stack the deck in my favor," she taunted.

"Nonsense. I'll play the Northbound Gnome."

"And I'll play the Turnip Knight, who can recruit your Gnome to my side."

"Blast! I'll play the... ummm... the Ladder of Discombobulation. We will now swap hands."

If you're having a hard time following, don't worry. Not even the dictionary could help anyone understand this game.

"Not so fast! I counter with the Stubborn Banana Peel, that cancels the Ladder's effect."

"*Squeak...*" I lamented.

"Silence, Gunnar, I'm trying to concentrate. I have the Two-Headed Rooster."

"That won't do you any good, synce I'm playing the Blacksmyth of Tyme. That means this round is myne! EEE-HEE-HEE!"

I don't want to say that my confidence in my employer was shaken, but as Mindy took her turn shuffling the deck, I began preparing my mind for the possibility of a lifetime as a tree-dwelling rodent. He too, appeared to be nervous as he carefully examined his cards, and made his opening move of the final round.

"The Onion of Perspective," He announced.

"Ohh, interesting!" Mindy said. "A worthless card on its own whych requires a lot of luck to use properly."

"I'm aware of how the Onion works. Maybe you believe that I'm luckier than you and you'd like to forfeit?"

"I've never stood down from an Onyon before, and I'm not about to start tonyght! I'll play the Bothersome Bryck Wall."

"A defensive play. Feeling nervous, are we?"

"I play to wyn, you beardy old oaf. Take your turn."

"Very well. The Soldier of Fortune."

"EEE-HEE-HEE! How predyctable! I'll just ruin your whole plan wyth the Moon in June card. Now your Soldier of Fortune is useless."

"You think you know what I'm planning, do you?"

"It's obvious. An Onion and Soldier combynation is one of the oldest trycks in thys game."

"But what if I play the Quiche Prince?"

Suddenly, the witch was as puzzled as I was, that is to say, hopelessly confused.

"But, but... that would only work if you somehow had..."

Mortenson held up a card with a picture of a constipated-looking chimpanzee on it, and proudly declared, "The Explosive Ape?"

"NOOOOO-HO-HO!" wailed Mindy.

"Yes, indeed! The blast from the Explosive Ape eliminates all cards on the table, except for The Onion of Perspective and Soldier of Fortune, who are protected by a pardon from the Quiche Prince. With the Moon in June destroyed, I've won!"

I had no earthly idea what Mortenson had just said but seeing the look of victory on his face and the agony of defeat on the witch's was good enough for me, and I chittered with joy. The old man stood triumphantly, and Mindy slumped in her chair.

"Now, Myndelom, a deal's a deal. Undo all of the spells you've placed over us tonight."

"Fyne, fyne, fyne! Squirrel-boy, get back into your shyrt and I'll fyx you up."

I climbed inside of the pile of clothes, and I couldn't see what she did, but I suddenly felt my body expand to fill them out. My fur and tail contracted back into my body, and once again, I was human. I lay there on the floor, dizzy and perplexed at what I'd experienced in the last twenty minutes.

"Gunnar, son!" Mortenson cried. "Let me help you up, lad. There you go. Tell me, how do you feel, lad?"

I rubbed my temples and got my balance back, saying, "I feel peachy, although I still have this wild cravin' for acorns."

"It'll pass. And you, witch, you've lifted your enchantments?"

"Yes, yes, the forest is back to normal. As normal as it was before, at any rate. If you head strayght out from my front door, you'll reach Raspberry Hyll."

"Very good. Come, Gunnar, we haven't a moment to lose."

As we exited the hut, I heard Mindy call after us, "Oh, do vysit agayn sometyme. This was such marvelous fun! EEE-HEE-HEE!"

We returned to the woods, and marching along, Mortenson threw his beard over his shoulder again.

"Did you know that would work, sir?" I asked.

"Of course, a witch can never resist a game of Ochre King's Court."

"It's a lucky thing that you played so well, I reckon."

"Absolutely right, my boy. Especially since she was cheating. But we can't dawdle. There are only fifteen minutes to midnight!"

# Chapter 34

Mr. Mortenson and I rushed desperately through the forest. We were only minutes away from midnight, but there was no telling how much further we had to go to reach Raspberry Hill and the Curiosity Shop. The run-in with Ethel Myndelom had cost us much of our precious time, and now the sands of the hourglass were dwindling to nothing.

If not for the old man—and it was not his fault—I could have made a mad dash to get there in time. His age slowed him down considerably, and try as he might, he wasn't able to run. Even though I was carrying both shovels and the lantern, he had to hobble with his cane and complained about the pain in his joints.

"Sir, maybe you can give me the keys and the sack o' gold and I'll run to the shop to pay the Landlord?" I offered.

He wheezed, "No... the Landlord will be... *gasp*... coming for me, wherever I am."

"Is there some way we can move faster, then? Can you perform some magic that'll get us there, or allow us to fly, or anythin'?"

"No, I can't do that... There is a magic carpet in my storeroom, but I've been neglecting to beat out the old dusty thing, so even if we had it with us it unfortunately couldn't fly. We just need to... *Cough! Cough!* Keep moving." At that moment, his eyes lit up with hope. "But wait! We're in luck!" he sauntered over, panting as he went, to yet another old tree.

Its trunk was twisted around in a spiral pattern all the way to the leafless branches, which curled into jagged spirals.

Fearing another encounter with unhelpful vegetation, I asked, "It ain't more chat-talky mushrooms, is it?"

"No, better than that. It's a warped tree! Remember I told you that every plant and fungus in the forest is connected by a network of roots?"

"Yeah, it's how they communicate."

"Well, some trees—magically infused, ancient ones such as this—have the ability to transport matter by the same mechanism, to other warped trees like it. We'll just need to convince it to help us." Mortenson knocked on the tree's trunk, and from between eyelids made of bark, a pair of uneven, wooden eyes slid drowsily open.

"Hrrmm... Wot, wot, wot? Who goes there?" it said with a mouth that was wide and crooked, following the crevices of the papery bark that was peeling off at the lips. Additionally, it had a broken stump of a branch between its eyes which it twitched as if it were a nose it could sniff with.

"Oh, it's a couple of humans," it mumbled. "Why, I haven't seen any humans around here in an ice age. Not for many, many rings. Why, I remember one season... *yawwwwn*... that there were... ZZZZZZZ..." The elderly plant winked his eyes and began to snore.

Mortenson shouted, "Sir! Wake up, sir!" before it could doze off back to sleep.

"Urgh! What now? Human, why did you wake me up? If I don't get at least eight decades of sleep, I'll be very cranky in the morning."

"I'm terribly sorry, sir, but we are in desperate need of your assistance. We urgently need to get back to Raspberry Hill."

"Where, now? Oh, right, that new human settlement."

"It's been there for a century and a half," Mortenson pointed out.

"From my perspective, that's very recent. I can remember a time when there were no humans around here at all. In fact, when I was just a sprout, there were—"

Mortenson interrupted, "Yes, I'm sure you have a wealth of fascinating history that you could tell us, but if we don't get back to the town, you see, and in no uncertain terms, I will die."

"So what?" grumbled the tree. "You humans cut down many of my friends and neighbors to build your little town. Why should I care if one or two of you are cut down in return? It's no bark off my trunk."

"I can promise to return later and listen to your whole life story, if you please."

The tree responded by rolling its eyes and scoffing, which sent little splinters flying into our faces. He grumbled, "That promise is hollower than a termite-infested log. You won't be coming back here, and it's not like I can come after you to make good on it. I haven't moved from this spot since I landed here as a wee baby acorn."

"Is there anything I could give you to persuade you to help us?"

"What on Earth could we possibly bribe a tree with?" I wondered aloud.

"Hmmmm..." pondered the old tree. He turned sinister, and said, "There is one thing that you humans possess that I'd like. Something refreshing, that I have not tasted for ages. Something you all carry within you and can't live without. The sustenance of *all* living things. *That* is what I crave."

"And... what exactly is it that you want?" Mortenson apprehensively inquired.

I was horrified to think of the sacrifice that the tree was about to ask of us. The price for magic such as this may be dramatically steep. Did it want blood? Flesh? Our very lives?

The tree's lips curled up into a wicked sneer as he demanded, "Air from your lungs."

The old man and I looked at one another, puzzled, and

mostly relieved. "That's it?" I inquired, dumbfounded. "You just want us t'breathe on you?"

"Yes, that's what I desire! Fresh respiration, the very foundation of life!"

"Mind if I ask why?"

The tree calmed down from its excitement, and levelly explained, "You see, it's like this. You know how humans will travel from the city to the country for some fresh air? It's the same with me, except I can't go anywhere. It gets so stuffy here in this crowded forest, breathing the same air as all these other whippersnapper saplings. So, oblige me, please, with some fresh air from your lungs, and I'll transport you to Raspberry Hill."

This was not the oddest, or even the most unpleasant task I had undertaken that evening, but it was perhaps the most uncomfortable and awkward. Mr. Mortenson and I stood on opposite sides of the ancient trunk, and took turns blowing on it, all the while the old tree was muttering things like, "Ah, lovely... how refreshing!" and "I feel younger than I have in centuries!"

After a few minutes of this embarrassing work, the tree announced, "All right, I'm satisfied. Thank you both. Best air I've respirated since, oh, that one time back in the summer of the perpetual rains..."

Not wanting to get caught up in nostalgic waxing, Mortenson insisted, "So you'll deliver us to the closet warped tree to Raspberry Hill, then?"

"Hmm? What did you say? Oh, right, right, silly me. I'd forget my trunk if it weren't attached. Just pass through my mouth, and you'll be there."

His lips separated, and with a creaking wooden sound like an old pirate ship, his lower jaw descended to the forest floor. The opening was just big enough for a person to crouch through. Within the portal of his mouth, I could see the houses, the buildings, and the streets of Raspberry Hill.

"Marvelous!" exclaimed Mortenson. "We are much obliged to you, my wooden friend. Come, Gunnar, we are only minutes away from midnight!"

"Oo ehcung," said the tree with his mouth wide open.

Stepping through the maw of the ancient tree, we were transported to the edge of the woods, and deposited from the mouth of another warped tree that loomed over the town. The bark closed up behind us with another groaning scrape.

"Amazing!" I exclaimed. "We just crossed the whole darn forest in an instant! But... that begs the question, why we didn't use that in the first place instead of goin' on such a long hike?"

"No time to marvel and wonder," insisted Mortenson. "Let's just say it was a character-building exercise and leave it there. Okay? Midnight is nearly here!"

 # Chapter 35

WE CUT A STRAIGHT line across the grassy field at the edge of the forest back to town and reached the Curiosity Shop. As we approached the front door, I could see Ysabel through the window, scratching urgently at it and shouting something that was muffled by the glass and wood. As Mortenson turned the key to let us into the shop, we heard a dreadful sound from the top of the hill.

BUNG!

It was the chiming of the church's steeple bells, striking the hour of midnight.

"Blast it! We're almost there and almost out of time!" He spluttered, finally getting the door unstuck and pushing it open.

BUNG!

Inside, Ysabel was pacing and flicking her tail in agitation.

"You're late!" she yowled. "You were supposed to be here no later than 11:30 to fill my food dish. I need it to be full in case I get peckish in the middle of the night. Oh, and your yearly payment is due now."

"We were waylaid by circumstance!" Mortenson replied, hobbling to the door of the storeroom. "I'll explain everything later."

"Oh, I don't care for an explanation, I'd just like a salted herring as recompense."

"Shush!"

BUNG!

The old man took out the rusted iron key and opened the storeroom door. All of the monster crates, though still held in place by their chains, were rattling violently. Were the monsters contained within afraid of what was coming, or mocking the position we were in? I thought the former far more likely.

"Gunnar, help me with this," Mortenson ordered, indicating a wooden chest sandwiched between two chained crates on the bottom tier of the shelf nearest to the door.

BUNG!

I grasped the handle on one side, and he the opposite. I cried out loud with the strain of lifting it. The crushing weight of the chest made hoisting it off of the shelf and onto the floor a Herculean task.

BUNG!

"Ready?" I asked. "We'll lift on three. One, two, three!"

I strained, groaning as a burning pain radiated through the muscles in my arms and back. I was able to raise my end an inch above the floor, but the old man was too frail to lift his side at all. He managed to make a sickening cracking noise and yelped before collapsing next to it.

BUNG!

Hoisting himself up to a strained crouch on the edge of the chest, my employer wailed, "It's no use. I can't lift it."

"By thunder, we'll drag it, then!" I roared. "Come 'round to this side."

BUNG!

Mortenson joined me on the doorway-facing side of the chest, and we gripped the handle tightly, dug in our heels, and yanked with all the might we could muster. I began to sweat, and the droplets ran down my face, stinging my eyes. However, the pain that encompassed my entire body had to be ignored as we struggled to drag the box of treasure.

BUNG!

Ysabel climbed up on top of the chest and hopped madly up and down, shouting, "Quickly, quickly! He's almost here."

Mortenson yelled at her, "That isn't helping at all, you fickle feline!"

"Okay, fine. I suppose this once I'll step down from my supervising duties to help with the leg work."

BUNG!

She hopped to the back of the chest, gripping the boards of the floor with her claws, and pushed with her head. Since the weight of this treasure was many, many times that of the tiny cat, the effort contributed very little, overall. The gesture was appreciated, however.

BUNG!

By our combined strength, the chest scraped its way through the storeroom door, leaving a trail of deep scuff marks in the floorboards behind it.

"Hurry, to the front," Mortenson shouted.

BUNG!

We had nearly reached the front door, groaning and crying out with every pull, choking for breath and coughing from the exertion of strength. With the last ounce of strength I felt I could summon, I lifted the chest and heaved. It settled by the front door just as the final bell chimed.

BUNG!

Suddenly, the front door was blasted open by a powerful gust of wind, nearly causing it to fly off its hinges. It swept through the store with a furious howl and knocked Mortenson and I to the ground, along with much of the merchandise from the shelves. Ysabel's fur stood on end, and she zoomed behind the checkout counter to hide.

After several moments of this chaotic maelstrom, it died down a little and I stopped rolling across the floor. I unbraced my head, turned toward the door, and faced the imposing figure that was now looming in the doorway.

It was Him.

Chapter 36

THE LANDLORD WAS MASSIVE, filling the frame of the doorway and allowing not a micrometer of leeway around him. His head, almost totally out of view and shrouded by darkness, rose above the top of the jambs. The only part of it that was visible was a bone-white chin, as pointed as a knife. Fog rolled in from behind him and enveloped his body.

He wore a simple black cloak, made of a material so dark that not only did it not reflect light, but seemed to absorb it completely. Even the brightness of a star in supernova was no match for its ravenous blackness. It was not merely dark; it was the *source* of darkness.

Mortenson tried to stand but couldn't. His cane had been knocked away from him and lay far out of his reach. He crawled on his hands and knees, then knelt before the Landlord, beard flapping like a banner in the wind. It was all I could do to pathetically lay on the floor in total awe of the fearsome specter that stood before us.

The old man declared, "I've done it, your lordship. It's all here in this chest, what I owe you this year. Take it and be satiated."

The Landlord, without a motion of the head, extended an enormous arm out from the right side of his cloak. The size of it was thrice that of an ancient Olympic wrestler, with skin that was pale white, and chalky. It reached out and picked up the chest in a single gargantuan hand.

He brought the treasure up close to his torso, unveiled

another massive hand on his left, and with it, pinched the lid to wrench it open. It effortlessly snapped off, and the lock went clattering across the floor. The gold, jewels, and other priceless treasures, which would have otherwise sparkled dazzlingly, had all of their splendor sucked out by the presence of the Landlord.

He weighed the chest in his hand, and then stuck out a club-sized finger to count the contents. It appeared that he was double-checking. He seemed to have found that something was missing.

The Landlord's chin turned, and he glared menacingly at Mortenson from unseen eyes. A deep, rumbling growl rose from him which rattled the windows. A sinking feeling of doom overpowered me, and I feared that all hope was lost.

"Oh, wait!" the old man cried out, removing the small sack of gold from his coat pocket, and holding it up in the Landlord's view. "I nearly forgot about this, heh heh..."

The landlord took the sack between his thumb and forefinger, causing Mortenson to recoil in terror. He set the sack on top of the treasure heap and weighed the horde again. This time, the heft of it seemed to satisfy him, and he relaxed his shoulders.

The specter then reached into the pile with his fingers and plucked out a single gold dollar coin, which he flipped onto the floor with a snap of his fingers. It clinked and clattered, rolled across the floor, spun around and finally came to rest head's side up. The crowned profile of Liberty faced up at us.

Our change.

Lastly, the Landlord raised the sleeve of his cloak and placed the treasure chest inside it. He said absolutely nothing as he turned to depart. Not a noise, or even a single gesture was offered as he dissolved into the blackness, taking the wind and fog along with him.

We were left with nothing but silence, then. My boss and I remained on the floor, each of us staring miles away, panting and refusing to untense our bodies lest we do so prematurely. I didn't know what to say. I didn't want to say anything.

It took the re-emergence of Ysabel from behind the counter to break us from our stupor.

"Wow!" she exclaimed. "That was a close call, wasn't it?"

Mortenson shook himself and made his way toward his cane to help himself up. "It certainly was," he mused as he rose to his feet. Stepping over to the gold coin, he picked it up, examined it, and said, "One dollar over. That's closer, I think, than I've ever come before."

He dropped the coin into his coat pocket.

I helped myself up and asked, "Is the Landlord gone?"

"Yes, we won't see him again. Until next year, that is, when the rent will be doubled."

"Doubled!?" I shrieked.

"Yes, that's how it is with him. Every year, for many years now."

"Mr. Mortenson, sir, will you please tell me what in tarnation the Landlord truly is? After all, I've seen him in person now and survived, so I reckon you owe me an explanation."

"No, son, I don't believe I do. I won't ever tell you. You surprise me; I would think seeing him up close and knowing the situation I'm in would be enough to dissuade your curiosity."

"Maybe I'm dissuaded from workin' here at all. That's what you wanted, ain't it? That's what this whole night was s'posed to do."

"Gunnar, son..."

"No! You've been deliberately keepin' secrets from me all day, keepin' me in the dark, even when there was danger and peril. If that's the way it's gonna be here, then congratulations. You got your way. I don't wanna work for you anymore."

I glared at the old man, standing defiantly against him. He simply gazed back at me with sad, tired, milky-blue eyes.

"Lad," he muttered after a moment, "come with me. There's something I want to show you."

"What is it?"

"Only one more surprise, and this time, it won't be troll droppings, mischievous witches, or anything of that nature. It's on the roof. We'll fetch my telescope and climb up there. If you'll allow me, there's one more thing I want to show you tonight."

I considered what I had been through, what I had said, and what the old man had told me. Despite my anger, he seemed to be in earnest, so I decided that I would hear him out and give him one last chance.

Chapter 37

And so, up on the roof we went. In the alleyway between the Curiosity Shop and Tumble's Drugstore, there was a steel ladder that ascended to it. Before we started our climb, I noticed an armadillo rooting around in the trash there, which I surmised to be Tumble's pet, Spot. For reasons I couldn't quite explain, seeing him there was comforting to me.

We climbed onto the roof, me behind Mr. Mortenson with a telescope case slung across my back. The combination of the calm night breeze and the gentle choir of chirping crickets served to cool down my temper somewhat. By the time we had reached the top, I was feeling far more reasonable.

The witch's spell that had caused the prior overcast had cleared, and once again the night sky was the sort that would inspire painters and poets. The Milky Way arced overhead like an azure ribbon among the sea of stars that shimmered and winked at us.

I helped the old man set the telescope up on its tripod. He adjusted the apparatus while muttering some astronomical calculations, and finally, settled on a point in the heavens and aimed the telescope toward it.

Peeking through the eyepiece, he said, "Ah-ha! There it is. Take a look through there, lad, and tell me what you see."

I did so, and among the many glittering dots in the black and cobalt sky, there was a pale crimson speck that glowed brighter than the others.

"I see a bright red star," I answered.

"That's no star, lad," Mortenson explained. "*That* is the planet Jupiter. The fifth planet from the Sun in our solar system. By far the largest of all of them, and by a pretty wide margin, too. A giant made entirely of gas, soaring through the universe hundreds of millions of miles away from where we stand right now."

"Mr. Mortenson, you didn't bring me up here just for an astronomy lesson. What's the point o' this?"

"The point is, son, that the universe is unfathomably huge, and hides secrets so numerable and so impenetrable that we may never discover all of them. That doesn't stop people from trying, though. Curiosity led man to invent the telescope so that they could look closer into the mysteries of the cosmos, and we discover more and more as we keep making bigger and better ones. I know I'll never get to go to Jupiter, but maybe someday, mankind will devise a method to travel there, and will be able to satisfy their curiosity.

"Curiosity is a good thing. It drives discovery and invention, and it led you to me, and to a world of secrets that not even *I* have a complete knowledge of. It's a good thing it did, too, because I couldn't have survived this night without your help. Stay curious, lad, don't give up, don't let anyone tell you that you're wasting your time, and the answers to your questions will be revealed to you.

"You will encounter obstacles in your quest for knowledge, and I'll be honest, sometimes that will be me. There are just some secrets I hold that I'm not willing to reveal on my own. You're a bright young man, though, not to mention persistent. Those qualities will help you discover the truth someday. There's a lot that I will teach you, as well."

"Are you sayin'...?"

"I'm saying that I want you to keep working for me, as my assistant, after school on weekdays and Saturdays. I thought that I didn't need an assistant, and that I could get you to change your mind by taking you along with me tonight. It's true what you said before. I was confident that the strangeness and danger would discourage you. What happened instead was you ended up changing *my* mind. You displayed a tremendous amount of bravery, quick thinking, and strength of character tonight. Here..."

He reached into his pocket and removed the gold dollar. Holding it between his thumb and forefinger, he took my hand, placed it in my palm, and then closed my fist around it.

"Your pay for a hard day's work. You take that home now and think on what I've said to you, and if you decide you still want to work for me, I'll see you tomorrow afternoon."

I turned the coin over and over in my hand, feeling the weight of it. Nodding at the old man, I silently pocketed it. Nothing more was said between us before I helped myself down the ladder, and taking side streets, made my way back home.

The neighborhoods of Raspberry Hill were utterly noiseless. It seemed like the entire world was asleep now, save for me. Everyone dreamed comfortably in their beds, totally unaware of the danger and wonder that existed right outside their doors. Shoot, only days before I had known no more than any of them.

Now I had seen the elephant, as Mr. Tumble put it.

If they knew what I knew now, what would they make of it? Let alone if they knew what I knew I didn't know. Would they see it through to the end or say *no thanks, I think I'll return to the comfortable ignorance I enjoyed before*? What would anyone else have done in my place?

How would Herbie have handled it? Was I any braver or brighter than the next adolescent? I wondered what my sisters might have done, or others I had met in town. Mr. Tumble, now there was a man who would be totally lost if he were in my place. And Ms. Pearson, she didn't have enough curiosity in her to look out of her own back door. Although I had to admit, she would probably have stood a chance against Ethel Myndelom, or imploded under the mass of their combined stubbornness. What would Pa or Ma have done?

Oh, shoot!

How in blazes was I supposed to explain to my parents why I was coming back past midnight, and covered in filth? I definitely couldn't tell them the truth. It didn't matter if they believed me or not. Either way, they would forbid me from going anywhere near the Curiosity Shop again.

There was no way around it, I was going to have to sneak back in.

Chapter 38

I ARRIVED AT MY house, noticing that the gas lamps were still on in the library. My parents were indeed still awake. The window had been left wide open to allow fresh air into the room, and creeping soundlessly through the grass, I sat under the windowsill, and eavesdropped on my parents' conversation.

"I can't take any more of this waitin', hon," my mother sobbed. "I'm worried sick about Gunnar!"

Pa replied, "Calm down, Mary, don't getcher self too worked up."

"And how in the dickens are you so calm? Don't you care that our boy is missin'?"

I had expected my father to say the worst about me, then. He and I had always had a hard time seeing eye-to-eye. I figured he would just say something like, *'Well, the boy's big enough to look after 'imself. If he wants to go out on his own, let 'im.'*

Then he surprised me.

"O' course, I care," he said, gentler than I'd ever heard him speak before. "He's *my* son, too. I don't always understand 'im, but I know that he's a good boy, and wouldn't be out causin' trouble, an' he's strong, too. My heart ain't made o' stone, y'know. I worry about 'im all the time. I know I can be hard on 'im, but it's only because I want 'im to make the right choices and succeed in life. So that's how come I can stay calm; because I trust our boy."

"Either way, it's way past midnight. We should call the

police."

Pa agreed, and the pair of them left the library for the kitchen, where our telephone was.

I was beside myself, then, sitting in the grass outside of my home. Never in a million years would I have expected *my* Pa to have a soft side. The guilt started to gnaw at me, and I wanted to curl up into a ball and cry, but if I knew what was good for me, I would have to get a move on.

I hoisted myself through the window and removed my boots so that they wouldn't make noise or leave muddy footprints on the floor. My secret passageway was behind one of the bookshelves in the library, and I carefully tiptoed to it. Feeling around the backside, I found the latch that held it closed, and it swung open when I pulled it.

Creeping inside and holding my breath, I slowly shut the door behind me. So careful was I that a deer standing next to it wouldn't have detected the microsonic *click* it made. I thought I was in the clear, until I turned around and stumbled over the candle holder that I had left there the day I discovered the passageway.

The loudest sound in the world is the one that gets you caught.

"*What was that racket!?*" I heard Pa growl from the kitchen, followed by the bell of the phone being slammed on the receiver. Angry, stomping footsteps approached.

Yikes! Forsaking stealth, I raced down the secret hallway, up the ladder, and through the other passageway. Feeling my way around in the dark, I bumped knees, stubbed toes, and jammed fingers, uttering curses that I won't reproduce here in print.

I finally came to the inside of my closet and could hear my parents racing up the grand staircase. As quickly as I could, I tossed my dirty clothes on the floor, remembering to take out the gold dollar so I wouldn't lose it, and put on a night-shirt.

The footsteps were right outside my door, now, and I threw myself into my bed and under the covers. At that instant, the doorknob turned, and my bedroom door swung open. My parents turned on the gas lamp in my room, and I pretended to have just been woken up from a deep sleep.

"Who's there!?" Pa roared as light flooded the room.

"Wha...? Ma? Pa? What time is it?" I said with pretend grogginess, squinting my eyes.

"Gunnar!" they both exclaimed. Ma sat on the bed right by my side, and Pa stood beside her.

"Lord have mercy, son!" he huffed. "Have you been here the whole time?"

"Y' missed supper, and we ain't seen or heard hide nor hair o' you all evenin'!" Ma scolded with her arms crossed. "Where have y' been?"

"Oh, I didn't mean to worry you. I got myself a job in town."

"A job?" my father replied with a mix of disbelief and intrigue.

"Where at?" demanded Ma.

"At a store in town. I'm workin' as a shop assistant after school, and today was my first day. It was really busy, with lots to do, so I was kept pretty late. Boss fixed us supper, and then I came home, let myself in, and went to bed. I didn't want to disturb you." It was at least *basically* the truth.

Ma was not convinced. She asked, "You spent the whole day workin'? Don't tell your mother no lies, now."

I produced the gold dollar I had earned and proudly displayed it for them. "See?" I explained. "I made a whole dollar at work, there's the proof."

"Huh, a dollar a day ain't too bad for your first job," Pa mused.

"And why is it in bed with you?" Ma questioned.

"I, er... y'see..." I stammered to buy some time to weave another excuse. "This is sorta embarrasin'... I, um... I felt so good about earnin' my first dollar that I kinda fell asleep lookin' at it."

"Well, that's fine, my boy," Pa beamed, as if this were

something everyone did, and was too proud of his employed offspring to question it.

Ma wasn't totally satisfied yet, however. She said, "Okay, I believe you, Gunnar. But you shouldn'ta kept us in the dark like that. We were worried to death about you."

For this, I felt truly guilty, and apologized, "Sorry, Ma. I'll let you know where I'm gonna be in the future."

"You'd better. Good night, Gunnar. I love you," she said, kissing me on the forehead and standing to leave.

"Night, son. I'm mighty proud o' ya," Pa said as he followed her out, turning out the light and closing the door behind him.

Kept in the dark. The phrase echoed in my head as I laid alone in the moonlit night. I had used the phrase more than once that night while accusing old man Mortenson of the same. It seemed that I was accumulating my own collection of secrets now, just as he did.

I reflected on the events of the evening. So much danger, what with a towering troll, a wicked witch, and beings from beyond the mortal realm. Mortenson's Curiosities was certainly not your average sundry shop. Should I really go back to work there?

There was danger, yes, but there were also so many unanswered mysteries. And there was so much joy in discovering their answers. I knew if I stuck with it, there would be more experiences like capturing the Squonk, discovering magical artifacts, and getting swept up in a fantastic adventure. Looking back at the evening, that's what it had been.

A fantastic adventure.

Mortenson, you *are* a crafty old spider, and you snagged me. You knew I wouldn't be able to resist the urge to return to unravel your web further. I'd be back the following day, ready to pry further into the world of magic and mysterious creatures. I vowed to myself then that I would never stop trying to find all the answers to my questions.

And so, kind reader, you now know how it was that I

came to work for Levi Mortenson at the magical Curiosity Shop. Do you still find it impossible to believe? You should hear about the adventures we had after that! Perhaps I shall relate them to you at a later time. For now, I will leave you with these parting words.

Stay curious. Don't let anyone try to tell you that there is any mystery that is out of your reach, because those who seek knowledge will find it.

And now, I lay down my pen until next we meet.

Book, return to your place on the shelf.
Clop!
Clop!
Clop!

ABOUT THE AUTHOR

Josh Berliner was born in 1993 and grew up in the Metro Detroit area of Michigan and has been writing stories since he was a little kid. He earned a Bachelor's in Applied Arts from Central Michigan University in 2015 and then a Computer Information Technology degree from Schoolcraft College in 2019 (because the Landlord *must* be paid). *Cryptid Currency* is his first novel. He lives happily near the coast of Lake Michigan with his wife and cat.